TRAIL OF THE WARRIOR

A Fable of Hope

R.H. PFEIFFER

All proceeds from sales of this book until January 2020 go to benefit a 501(c)(3), Families and Children Together (FACT, Inc.) a Not for Profit in the State of Kansas.

First published in 2018 by
WIL PUBLISHING
www.wordsinlight.org

Edited by Heather Spaur & Diane Potts

Cover Model: Tyler Krei

Library of Congress Cataloging in Publication Data Pending

ISBN: 978-0-9994886-0-7

Designed in the United States of America

Dedicated
to the
GLORY OF GOD
as we understand him
and to
THE ADDICT
who continues to suffer

Let the Warrior in all of us
battle against the forces of our lives.

Cindy, my love, thank you.

CONTENTS

AUTHOR'S NOTE

Have you ever thought, I hope I have the courage to get this done?

I see the characters of Liza, Joe, and Rosie as great healers. As an author, I will capture for you their insight, hope, and tenacity in a way that will compel you to embrace your own courageous living.

These three are put in the midst of a recovery need by their son and son-in-law, Charlie. Charlie is an Afghanistan War veteran, who upon entering recovery, becomes an even deeper story of human need to escape addiction. This book discusses meaningful recovery and the challenges that life brings. Addiction affects us all.

Charlie's addictive behavior is interrupted by the presence of a dog named Rosie. The consequences from that event spark a movement of destiny through a higher power in his journey of recovery.

This book creates touchable interaction of a higher power at work through the mystery of human life and spirit, ignited by the appearance of Rosie as she helps lead Charlie through recovery.

This book highlights and grows hope in a garden of recovery.

PROLOGUE

This is what Charlie had been waiting for. The house was quiet. The girls were asleep. As if his life depended on the results, Charlie began again to write in his journal.

Charlie wrote...

If you battle with addiction, there is no doubt that your life and very soul will fight with John Barleycorn to the end. There are two paths. One is filled with anger, resentment so deep with guilt that the worst of that shame becomes routine and the burden all yours. If your life is taken down this path, you believe that your life is worth nothing, and that becomes your reflection on the world around you. By action, the practicing addict who beats his wife and his children shows that a substance is more important than life.

The second path is one of confrontation between the denial of an out-of-control life and the relentless search of how to restore yourself as your warrior soul seeks recovery. The addiction is a brand upon your heart and though it may heal, the scar can never completely be removed. As an addict in recovery, you must learn your weapons of sobriety, keeping them close at hand and never again to lay them to the ground of blind denial.

John Barleycorn is willing to bring you an early death, if you by mistake listen to his seduction.

The waste of a drunken, drug-filled life is foolish.

An addict prays for clarity to examine that addictive scar and in the battle for sobriety, expecting nothing else, reflects hope and the kindness and goodness to heal others.

And, that is why I left Rosie, to heal others.

PART I: LIZA

CHAPTER 1: PRESENT DAY

October 2017

O ur father who art in Heaven, hallowed be thy name, thy kingdom come." Charlie did not know what had motivated him to say it, but it felt right. The pastor crumbled dirt on the grave, adding to the somber finality of the moment. As Charlie looked around at all the people, he wondered what had brought everybody here and was surprised that there were so many in attendance.

Liza continued the prayer. "Thy will be done on Earth as it is in Heaven."

Everyone began to speak in turn; all to say goodbye to Rosie. Weeks ago, Charlie knew her life must end. How could he ever let her go? She had heard so much over the years; listened, been a friend; delivered a lot of people from evil.

"Forgive us our debts as we forgive our debtors." Charlie continued to pray, as his mind flashed to the journal.

Joe, a weathered old Vietnam soldier, took his turn speaking about Rosie. His worn hat told a story, "Semper fi." Joe closed as he always did. "God will save your soul, AA will save your ass. Devil's in the brew."

Rosie, Charlie thought, you have no idea how many lives you have changed. Or maybe you do.

That rainy night when you appeared, John Barleycorn lost. Rosie won.

Finally, it was Charlie's turn to speak. So many emotions were swirling through him that he struggled to find the words.

So, he started at the beginning; the beginning that had saved his life so many years ago. "My name is Charlie and I am a recovering alcoholic and addict. In the bottom of a rain-filled ditch on a stormy night, Rosie arrived and saved my life."

Charlie spoke of his story of recovery. Then, as Charlie walked away from the grave, Joe put his arm around him.

Charlie turned to Joe and said, "I wrote in my journal last night about Zoey. She was my dog I lost when I was eleven."

Joe said, "Let's go read the journal over a cup of coffee."

From the journal, Charlie read...

"Zoey and I were always close. We were inseparable.
She awoke with me, ate with me, slept with me.

In hard times a bark, a growl, a lick made life less anxious. She made the family chaos easier to bear. It was as if some deeper force joined us together. I hoped to be her protector and hero.

Zoey was my angel and guardian. Zoey unselfishly gave of her calm presence, kindness, and loyalty. I spoke to Zoey always believing she understood. She wanted me to be a person that people respected.

Zoey taught me the worthiness of my hugs.

Zoey and I hid together; she taught me to be invisible when parties got out of hand.

There was a time when I thought Zoey was all I needed in life. She could teach me everything I needed to know. As Zoey became just a memory that memory became a treasure."

Now I know the world is only the visible aspect of God; What being a warrior does is cause a challenge by following the trail in search of a higher purpose for my life.

My recovery trail begins with a memo from my mother about that incredible dog, Rosie.

CHAPTER 2: MEMO

To: Staff and Patients   August 15th
From: Liza F., Lead Counselor
RE: Rosie (facility dog)

Be advised that starting today, a dog will be on campus. Straight from the Sheriff's custody, homeless and alone, a chocolate Labrador named Rosie has arrived here at the Southeast Kansas (SEK) Addiction Treatment Center. She is here on a trial period.

I am committed to seeing if having a dog at this facility is helpful; therefore, any concerns need to be brought to me as Lead Counselor.

This is a twelve step program, so please consider Rosie as a source of support as you work through the first five steps.

A journal is being provided for Rosie. If you have caught her being grateful, outgoing, supportive, or kind, her journal is the place to write it down. Rosie is available 24/7 to demonstrate the presence of a higher power among us.

In basic hope, love, and recovery, she will listen to all without judgement. She has sworn to confidentiality and will accept all in an honest and forthright manner. Any documentation of her abilities is welcome in Rosie's journal.

Rosie can only heal your heart and soul if you are willing to open up and let her into yours.

The courage of the first entry from Rosie's journal reads as follows:

Rosie,

Upon entering the treatment center, I felt no one in the world still cared for this soldier. Without a doubt you did. I don't know why, you must have known that I needed someone in my life. From day one you followed me. You helped me believe in myself again and you helped me get sober. The second day of my warrior's trail here, you followed me to the alley while I paced for over 30 minutes. You stayed right by my side the entire time and refused to return to the building until I did. I really believe what you were doing was making sure I didn't leave that day, and for that I thank you! You knew I was in a bad spot in my life. Without a word, you helped me rise above the addictive fog that hindered me from seeing and feeling anything. You helped me love, laugh, cry, and break away from the chains of sadness that held me captive. You brought comfort to those of us who are having the hardest time with this program. I thank you, my angel, for the comfort you gave me. Rosie, you make this place feel like home.

Charlie R.

CHAPTER 3: THE BEGINNING

Liza at Open AA meeting

My name is Liza and I am a very grateful, recovering alcoholic and addict. To be "recovering" means I once was powerless over alcohol and drugs. It is in that painful, unmanageable life that my story begins. Recovering means that one moment, one hour, one day at a time, I remain substance free. I will share the struggles, the hardships, the shame and guilt, and the eventual sobriety, recovery, and gratitude. Today, the pain swells in my throat. My tears are for my son, Charlie, who has relapsed. I am trying to be strong.

I am starting with my family history, because it certainly has a lot to do with how I perceived the world and how I perceived myself. I did not have a bad childhood. I had a father who worked a lot and I admired him very much.

My mother, however, had a very limited capacity to love, show love, or receive love. So, as a child growing up, the way I was disciplined was shame, verbal abuse, and lots of criticism. This affected my belief system. I thought there was something wrong with me. I thought that I was unlovable. I ended up searching most of my life for someone who could love me or change the way I felt about myself, not realizing it was my responsibility.

I learned to be very independent at an early age because all of my needs were shamed in my childhood. I started working as a carhop at 12 years old so I would not have to ask for help. Asking for help was difficult throughout my life. When I needed help, I felt shame.

The concept of surrender in recovery from addiction was difficult for me. Later, turning my life over to a higher power was extremely difficult, but proved to be life-saving. Now I find myself living powerless over my son's addiction. Life has come full circle and I am experiencing firsthand the pain my mother had to cope with over my addiction.

My life did not become unmanageable overnight. In high school I succeeded and I had a lot of friends. I dated in relationships with either an alcoholic or a male that I felt I needed to take care of. That is how I found my worth, by taking care of people. I felt like I had no value. In high school for the first time I experienced what alcohol could do for me.

An older person bought us some beer. The taste was awful, so I held my nose and drank four cans. I remember feeling this did something for me. I felt very confident.

I felt my inhibitions leave.

I liked the way it made me feel. It did something to me that my sisters never experienced. My sisters are not alcoholics.

I also experimented with smoking pot and taking acid. All things that kids back in the '70s experimented with, I tried.

My mom had a hippie for a daughter. I have an alcohol and opioid addict war hero for a son. He is suffering with the grace of a higher power; this power has done for me throughout my entire life what I cannot do for myself. I am very worried for my son. That son, Charlie, is missing.

I met my future husband in a hippie circle. I really looked up to him. I admired him. To be with him; I gave up my needs, wants, and desires. I was very happy in my job, but he wanted to live in California, so off we went. We stayed there for a while, then traveled around, then got married.

After that, we moved to North Carolina, which is where my first son, Robert Aaron Redon, was born. There was not a lot of alcohol or drug activity during that time. I did not drink or use drugs while I was pregnant. We then moved to Lawrence, Kansas, but eventually ended up in Hermosa Beach, California, where I worked in San Pedro for a while.

These moves were always about what my husband needed and wanted.

Wherever he was happy, I told him, I would be happy. I tried to believe it myself. He had a very negative view of the world. Making him happy became a mission.

While living in California our relationship turned abusive. I began walking on eggshells with my husband. I felt the same stress growing up with my mother.

Whatever I tried to do was never good enough.

I believed if I tried hard enough or wanted it bad enough, I could make a person happy. I could change them or make them love me.

I was unloveable. My core belief was a thinking error.

After the first episode of domestic violence, we moved back to Kansas.

My husband moved us out in the country. Domestic abuse flourishes with seclusion and isolation.

I was happy to be closer to my sister and parents.

Charlie Adam Redon was born here. Charlie who now finds himself powerless over the same addictions that once plagued me. Charlie is my second child.

"Charlie has been missing now for four weeks," Liza said, as she paused her story. Her eyes moistened, as she collected herself. Then she continued.

Now back in Kansas, the domestic violence, which had been mostly verbal, escalated to physical abuse.

I just hung in there, living in fear; believing something's going to be different. I always went to work and put on the front that everything was okay. I talked to no one.

I felt so much shame due to someone else's behavior. I was so embarrassed. I protected him.

People were starting to notice though. The abuse had become increasingly more difficult to hide. I was working at a law office. I would come to work with stories; that I was at a ballgame and a ball had hit me. I was so humiliated. I did not want to tell anybody. Back then people did not talk about those things openly. You did not hear about safe-houses or anything like that.

I was not doing a lot of drinking or drugs. I was just going to work, coming home, and trying to make everything okay. I never could. I moved out two or three times, but I always went back with the promise from him that things would change.

Unfortunately things did change, but not for the better. The violence grew worse.

I came home from work one night and everything that I owned was completely destroyed. I had nowhere to go and nothing to my name. I left everything behind, even my car.

A beautiful lady named Nicole took me and the boys into her home. To deal with all that pain and grief, we started going out on Wednesday nights to drink. I always drank differently than everyone else. I could not have just one beer. I would drink until I was so intoxicated that I could not even stand up. It was during this time that my husband started stalking me.

John would break into my home. If I was out with friends he would wait for me in the parking lot.

One night, he broke into the house and attacked Nicole and me. He left before the police came.

John always ran.

To avoid putting my friend in danger, I made the decision to leave Nicole's home. I got my own apartment.

My husband, John, would constantly torment me by breaking into my apartment. John terrified me. The police would come. I always refused to press charges; out of wanting to protect him, and fear that the violence would get even worse.

One night the police were called to my apartment. When they arrived, they found me unconscious.

The officer told me that if I did not press charges, they would. The officer confronted John that he had to be out of Bourbon County by April or he would go to jail. So he moved to Pittsburg, Kansas.

There is a purpose to everything. This happens in everyone's recovery story. As their lives become unmanageable, the emotional part of this illness gathers intensity. Choices are made. Once you make a decision, it is like jumping into the river's fast current: you flow onto the next event.

You will see this in not just my story, but in everyone's story of the progressive flow of addiction.

A short time later, I also moved to Pittsburg. In a thinking error again, I believed that leaving the past friends and problems behind and relocating to Pittsburg would serve as a sort of geographical cure, making everything okay.

Pride and memory had a fight and pride always wins.

For a period of time, there was no violence.

I took a job at a bar. Drinking every weekend, I often stayed out to early morning hours.

One night John came and he got violent at the bar. The next night, he would not let me leave to go to work. I called the police.

The officers made John leave my home and two days later he moved back to California. While John was in California, he continued calling me.

I had so much pain and guilt and it increasingly took more and more alcohol to take the pain away.

I realize today how unavailable and selfish I was with my children, only thinking about my own pain and my own needs.

There is a promise in the Big Book of Alcoholics Anonymous that says, "We will not regret the past, nor wish to shut the door on it."

The other promises have come true: "That we will intuitively know how to handle situations that used to baffle us. The fear of economic insecurity will leave us. We will suddenly realize that God is doing for us what we could not do for ourselves." Those promises have all come true. The regrets that I have are for hurting people along the way, though not knowing at the time how much.

Recovery has given me some insight into that as well, recognizing how my boys dealt with their pain. Robert masked his through achievement and Charlie with substance abuse.

My husband, still living in California, started sending me cocaine and methamphetamine through the mail.

I started selling to people I had met in Pittsburg.

I could not stand to be alone. The only way I could get rid of the loneliness, the guilt, and the shame was to drink and do more drugs.

Robert and Charlie needed me. I could not be the mother they needed. I dealt with my pain the only way I knew how: more drugs and drinking.

I got to know the circle in Pittsburg that was involved with drugs. I drank heavy. Every night when I got off work, I was surrounded by people who were my "using" friends.

I avoided my family. I was so ashamed of what I had become.

I could not stop what I was doing.

Addiction is that way.

CHAPTER 4: THE STRUGGLE

Liza

My life kept getting worse and worse. I tried to go back to college.

I tried to find something about me that I could feel good about. There seemed to be no one who cared. Being of no value was devastating, the emotional pain severe.

The alcohol and drugs I was using to mask the pain were slowly bringing the bottom up.

I found it increasingly difficult to function with everything that was going on at my house. The drug culture friends were running in and out all hours of the day and night. It was exhausting.

My precious children were living in a world of chaos and risk. My shame was only deepened by my denial of any problems. I reasoned that I had always been able to pay my bills and take care of myself, so everything was fine. I even had a car.

The only people who did not see my dysfunction were those I did drugs with. Robert and Charlie were collateral damage.

Shame is reflected on the faces of children you love and in the actions of family members that hang onto hope that something, anything, will touch your life and stop the madness of progressive addiction. Certainly, I feel that is where my mom and dad were.

Looking back now, I realize I was deaf and blind to my boys. I was an awful parent.

My husband and I got divorced, and I found myself in a new relationship with someone who drank as much as I did. I did not hang out with anyone who did not drink or use drugs. I did not want them questioning me. If they did, I kicked them out of my circle. No sober everyday people were allowed.

The whole time I was with this new boyfriend, Steven, I compared myself to him and thought, "I am not that bad." He was further progressed than I was, because he would get up in the morning and drink. Not me; I waited until night. Steven was unemployed. I worked in the bar every day. Comparing myself to him, I felt better.

One night, Steven wrecked my car and I became very upset with him. I gave him an ultimatum. He either had to go to treatment or he had to get out of my life.

I reasoned that if I could quit drinking for two weeks, then that would prove I did not have a problem.

Steven was the one with the problem. Towards the end of Steven's treatment, I would go to family day to visit him, reeking of leftover alcohol. The counselor would tell me,

"You need to look at your problem."

And I thought, "My problem?" I got really angry with my boyfriend and asked if he had been talking about me at the treatment center.

When Steven left treatment, he tried to stay sober. He had a sponsor and was doing what he was supposed to do, but I continued drinking and using. I remember thinking, "I cannot wait until he goes to an AA meeting." I started hiding and sneaking alcohol and drugs. I was not fooling him one bit.

I went to my first AA meeting on New Year's Eve with Steven. I remember thinking, "This is a great place for these people."

Still, I did not see how progressed my own disease had become. Denial is a powerful symptom of addiction. Denial tells you that you can quit anytime you want.

All along the way, I continued to believe that my two-week period of sobriety was proof that I did not have a problem. I continued to drink.

The selfish part of me was hoping that Steven would join me in drinking again.

I came home one day and he was acting very strange. The next morning when I woke up, he was drunk and high. After five months Steven had relapsed.

My children were home, so we all went out driving around Pittsburg and then cruised around in the country. He continued to drink and became violent. As I was driving down the road, he took his fist and cracked the windshield.

I told him our relationship was over. I would not live with the abuse and the terror a second time.

Steven packed up his things and moved out of my life, which accelerated his downward spiral; one that I was powerless to stop.

Even though our relationship was over, we had the same circle of friends, and we occasionally ran into each other. A few times, in moments of weakness, Steven would spend the night. I think that gave him false hope that we would resume our relationship.

This on-again, off-again relationship went on for several months, until I got involved with a man that my sister introduced me to. She apologizes to this day for that.

Immediately we had an attraction, an animal magnetism.

I remember thinking, "This guy has a car and a job!"

People I dated often lacked both.

Our relationship was exciting and electrifying and we dated for a really short time before we were married.

This second husband's name was Travis.

Travis had just gotten out of prison before we met and he was on probation.

Early on, we started doing drugs together and things got really bad. Not any physical abuse but awful, horrible emotional abuse.

During that time, there was a lot of infidelity on his part, which was very painful to me.

I felt shamed.

Guilt is a feeling that I did something wrong and I can do something about it, but shame is a feeling that there is something wrong with me, that I am flawed and defective.

The shame was disabling and I was only able to dissolve that feeling by more drinking and drugs.

Two months after I married Travis, Steven's parents knocked on my door. Steven had killed himself.

After the shock wore off, the guilt set in. This was all my fault. Why had I kept up a relationship with Steven, giving him false hope? The choices in our lives affect others.

I believed if I had quit drinking he would not have relapsed. His death was entirely my fault.

My shame and Steven's parents' comments sent me the same message.

The deep pain, shame, and grief turned me into an emotional wreck.

Trying to deal with the death of Steven and my cheating husband, Travis, I started drinking more and doing more and more drugs to numb the emotional pain.

I began partying every single night. I was putting Robert and Charlie in dangerous situations and hurting my family members.

My mom and dad were so worried about me. They even came to Pittsburg to intervene. I remember thinking, "What do they think is so bad? I have a job, I pay my bills. It is not that bad. Why do they think it is so bad?"

I was okay, but that is what denial is all about.

Then, the hammer came down. Things got worse. Ironically, not for me though. I lived on Denial Street in a filthy apartment near Walmart.

Travis' parole officer told him he had to go to treatment. Travis refused, unless I went with him. I was afraid that he would end up in jail if I did not go to treatment too.

That is how crazy my thinking was.

I went, but not for myself. I went to treatment to take care of him.

In my mind, I was NOT an addict.

My life full of tragedies, I kept my hands in front of my eyes, never contemplating the cost of addiction in my life.

I was driving through life in the dark with the headlights off... John's abuse, Steven's suicide, Travis' infidelities — all horrible events that I never equated to my own addiction.

I was okay, I did not have a problem.

I went to treatment with Travis because he needed to go.

In true addict fashion, I was already thinking about getting my first drink just as soon as we got out.

CHAPTER 5: ROCK BOTTOM

Liza

The first week I was in treatment, I slept a lot. I got up and went to therapy group. Travis had been sleeping with other women at the treatment center, so they asked him to leave. Unit staff wanted me to stay.

I told them I am not staying, I only came for him.

I started packing my stuff and told Travis that I was leaving with him. He told me he had a ride and I needed to find my own.

I quickly packed, then ran to the entrance in a panic. I was hurrying so he would not leave me.

I got down to the end of the stairs at the front of the treatment center just in time to see him drive off with his girlfriend.

He left me standing there. I cried my eyes out as all the

pain, abandonment, and rejection swept through me. I was without even a quarter to call anyone. I collapsed and prayed. Finally, I borrowed a quarter, called a friend, and went home.

I think now about how co-dependent I was. Anyone who says this is not a feeling disease is in denial and they have not progressed enough. It is such an emotionally painful illness.

I had finally hit my rock-bottom. Left standing outside of the treatment center, watching my husband drive away with his girlfriend, I felt so empty and alone.

I went home and cried myself to sleep, with a Bible across my heart.

I was exhausted, broken and lonely, with a heavy burden of hurt. A deep hurt that turned to anger then resentment. My disappointment all turned inward, pointing directly back at me.

I had finally become the rejected, abandoned, worthless person that I had always pitied and was so afraid of becoming. Emotionally, I was dead.

I had no concept of the disease I suffered with or the hope that recovery would bring.

My self-sufficiency had turned into insufficiency.

I did not even have any money for groceries. I dug around the house, in sofa cushions and under furniture, scavenging for quarters to buy some food. Then I walked to Walmart in a snow storm to get some.

As I was walking back, I sank to my knees in despair. The tears had long since dried up.

Thoughts started swirling through my head. "I have always had a car. I have always been able to take care of myself. Now look at me, I have gone as low as one can go."

I saw no way out of the mess that was my life. I was at a place of surrender. I am so fortunate that I did not die.

Too hungry, too lonely, too tired... and totally powerless over my addiction, I had no more to give. I had no more hope and no more desire to keep going.

I was done.

In that quiet moment, on my knees in fresh fallen snow, I realized that I must surrender in order to reclaim my life.

In that profound silence, as I surrendered everything, I had a realization of a higher power.

You do not know how much you need spiritual clarity until that is all you have.

There is another promise in the Big Book of Alcoholics Anonymous that reads, "No matter how far down the scale you have gone, you will see how your experience can benefit others, and I pray that you receive this gift at this open meeting tonight."

I began to think about what I had learned in Sunday School. I had seeds planted because my grandparents were very faithful Christians.

They had taken me to church throughout my childhood

and I had watched them pray and serve the Lord. I always knew that God was there, but I felt like there was something wrong with me and that I was unlovable.

It was a time in my life that I was so far down that the only place I could look was up. I did have the belief that my life had changed, so I called my little sister who is also a faithful Christian, and I let her into my life. She came to my house and prayed with me. She loved me and accepted me.

She accepted me.

My family was concerned for me, so she called my dad and they prayed for me too.

She said that when she was praying, she had a vision. "I saw you in deep waters and you were being tossed back and forth through the waters." She continued, "I saw the hand of God reach down from Heaven and pull you out of that water and He set you on a rock."

"You were standing on the rock and I told Dad you were going to be okay."

We all knew that it was my illness of addiction I was drowning in.

I reflected on my sister's vision, and slowly my life began to change.

The first steps of Alcoholics Anonymous came to life as I surrendered.

My parents did not know that I had left treatment until my sister told them. They showed up at my house and Dad tried to talk me into going back. I told him I would be okay without that.

My father brought out my son Charlie and asked him, "Would you like for your mama to go back to treatment?" Charlie said that he would. I realized then that was one thing that I never paid attention to, what the boys wanted or needed. It was then that I made the decision to go back.

My fallen war hero who helped save me, my Charlie.

"I told you that you had a problem. You have always had a problem!" my mother angrily shouted from across the table.

I saw my dad nudge her under the table. He told my Mom that they were going to take care of my boys while I was in treatment. I could tell she did not really want to. I understand now that she had no perception of what to do next.

I went back to treatment the very next day.

This time, I went for myself.

PART II: FAMILY

CHAPTER 6: SAVING CHARLIE

The greatest battles are won in the mind," Liza repeated to herself as she drove to work. The rural drive from Fort Scott to Girard was not long. The road was vacant of traffic and she liked that. The commute gave her those moments to think. To think about her own recovery; and about what she was going to accomplish that day at the SEK Addiction Treatment Center.

Liza was grateful for her recovery. The last four weeks had been emotionally exhausting. The past kept pressing into the present.

At the open Alcoholics Anonymous meeting last night Liza's friend had told her, "You are only as sick as your secrets." Liza had been invited to tell her story before Charlie went missing.

She met her obligation to speak at the open meeting; never having the breath fully returned to her lungs or the pain in her heart leave as she prayed for Charlie's safe return.

Charlie could be dead. Drugs and booze may have caused him to black out. Charlie was officially missing.

At the open AA meeting, Lisa's wiry five-foot-two body had stood tall and proud through out the entire presentation. Toward the end of her long talk, her gravelly voice had been even dryer than normal.

She spoke at the highest level of truth. She told her life story and the lessons learned. Over fifteen years had passed since that cold day she had knelt in the falling snow. In that spiritual moment, the first three steps of Alcohol Anonymous had come alive in her surrender.

Today, her life had once again become unmanageable due to the progressive addiction of her son, Charlie. His addictive behavior had again shown Liza how powerless she was.

SEK Addition Treatment Center had been a godsend for her. Established in 1991, it offered her a chance to repay the recovery world for the gift of her own life. A decade-plus years in recovery, she still saw recovery as a gift. Every day she worked her program. Those life lessons expressed from the heart are powerful gifts that heal others. She had worked herself from a case manager to a counselor to a supervisor to team leader, and now to the position of Lead Counselor, which she had been doing for the last five years.

Her involvement in direct client care had lessened, though she still counseled on family days. Family days were very important to her. She tried to bring insight to family members. Addicts are very disruptive to family living.

In a confrontation while drunk, Charlie had recently assaulted his father-in-law, Joe. Then he left town in a drunken, drug-filled daze. Charlie had vanished. Gone.

For weeks, Liza had struggled with the recent death of her ex-husband, John. Then Charlie disappeared, completely off the map.

There was so much going on in her life. John, who lived in California, had either committed suicide or been killed. That sent trauma into an already disturbed and opioid-addicted man: their son Charlie.

She refused to allow the death of her ex-husband and the struggle with her son to consume her. She must face her responsibilities head on today, just like every other day. She must knock the negative thoughts from her mind.

She decided to instead contemplate all the joy in her life; the recent birth of her granddaughter, Emma. The pressures of life, a new baby, and the death of his father were causing Charlie to unravel.

He was self-medicating to cope with a military service injury and his alcohol addiction had progressed rapidly.

The struggle now was to enter the treatment facility and do her job. As she made the last turn, driving past the hospital on the backside of the campus, she saw a sheriff's patrol car. This was not an uncommon event to see at the facility.

Often, patients were brought into the substance abuse treatment facilities by officers. Sometimes they were transfers to and from jail.

Today, there was just something about seeing the car that

brought dread to her heart.

Parking her car and getting out, Liza reached for her briefcase. "Things are going to be okay today," she reminded herself. "Things are going to be okay," she thought as she began walking towards the building.

A Sheriff's Deputy, Jess Redon, stepped out of the patrol car. Jess was her dead ex-husband's brother. He was a large man in full uniform, complete with gun, taser, and bullet-proof vest, making him seem larger than life.

His fists were balled up at his sides as he stormed towards her, and Liza could not help thinking, "What's his dry drunk problem, now?" Jess had long ago given up alcohol, yet he had no serenity about him. He was always ready for a fight. His resentments toward John and Charlie ran deep.

Liza had known that she had been a lousy parent at times. The struggle and the pain of that seemed to come and go. Certainly, helping others had helped to heal some of those old wounds.

Facing off with Jess and his large frame this early in the morning brought back a lot of fear and anxiety. Jess blamed Charlie's problems on her and John. With eight years between them, Jess and John still looked a lot alike. They could have been twins.

Those gut-level feelings of spousal abuse, vulnerability, and male disregard flooded through Liza and stopped her dead in her tracks.

"We have got Charlie," he shouted from 15 feet away as he walked towards her. "We have got your kid."

The man always looked like he was getting ready for a fight. There was no need for that right now. Liza had tried to shoulder the burden of raising Charlie and his older brother

Robert alone. She knew her failings.

Sobriety did not come for her until Charlie was twelve years old.

Robert had set his own path. Robert was succeeding in spite of her illness, but not so for Charlie. Charlie was failing.

Now, John, Jess' brother, was dead.

Bringing her back to the present, Deputy Jess bellowed, "Charlie was found in a gas station in Independence, Missouri and we got him on a transfer. The little shit is in our jail now. The officers up there said he was just plain out of it. The warrant from Joe's assault complaint came up, so the Independence Police Department held him for us."

Liza thought to herself, here comes that angry, dry drunk attitude again. Jess, I do not need your attitude. I do not need your crap. Liza kept quiet though; Jess was just too close and so damn big. Besides, we both knew John and I had failed Charlie.

She could not keep quiet any longer, "Jess, Charlie is a sick person. He needs to get well. He has an addiction and has relapsed. He is not a criminal needing to be judged by you."

This was his duty; that is the way Jess saw worthless druggies. So once again he was making the rules and confronting Liza. Jess felt bad about John on many levels. Losing a brother was not easy. Jess looked at the choices that John had made in his life, the drugs in his youth, then marrying Liza so young and having two children. John did so many drugs and he sold even more.

He had protected John as much as he could; maybe too much. Jess, as an older brother, had felt like John's father. Jess felt deep sorrow when John continued to destroy his life.

Jess had taken on a parenting role when he came back from

the Vietnam War.

Jess had white knuckled the war and once stateside returned to being sober. He had turned it all inward and just locked it all up inside. He had drank heavy for a while and then he just stopped. For Jess, this created a resentful dry drunk.

John should have just stopped too. He should have never started the drugs. He did not have a war he was trying to escape from. John got into constant trouble. Jess rescued him. That brother frustrated him. Why did he not just stop?

It really pissed him off that he now had to deal with Charlie, John's drunken son, too.

Where the hell was John, anyway? Dead.

Dead in California from an overdose. Maybe a bad drug deal? Who knows?

At this point, Jess did not even care. He had to take care of addicts his whole life, and he was sick of it.

No, there was no serenity in Jess. He was sober and that is where it stopped. He was an angry, resentful dry drunk.

Jess said, "Liza, he just needs to grow up. Grow up."

Liza replied, "Jess, he is not taking his father's recent death well. No matter what John was to you or me, he was still Charlie's father. He was blind to his failings. He lost his father."

Jess said, "Well Robert is doing ok. How come Charlie cannot? Maybe he could go back to school or something?"

"Jess you know Charlie struggled since coming back from Afghanistan. Plus he has a new baby and now he no longer has a father."

"Right, father. Bullshit," Jess shouted.

"Liza, here's the deal. He was wandering around with his car in a ditch near Independence, Missouri. I got him. Don't know why I would want him, but I got him. And he keeps mumbling stuff about being on a mission from the president. I do believe he is still coming down off of whatever crap he was on."

"Jess, is he safe?"

"Well, he is locked up."

Liza said, "Jess, just go through the normal protocols. Call someone in to assess him and treat him like you would anyone else."

"Well there is one more problem, Liza. He had a dog with him, a large reddish brown Labrador."

"Charlie does not have a dog, Jess."

"He does now and he says it is his."

"Where is this dog now?"

"The dog is in the back of my patrol car and I am taking her straight to the city pound. They will have to destroy the dog there."

"You are not going to destroy the dog! I will sort it out, Jess, just give me the damn dog."

"Well, Charlie calls the dog Zoey, not Damn." Jess laughed at his own joke. "The dog's name tag says Rosie, you can call the dog Damn or whatever you want, I don't care. Either way, you take the dog or it goes to the pound. Charlie is a mess, Liza. Between you and my brother, that kid is really screwed up."

Liza thought to herself, "I could not save my ex-husband, and I cannot fix my son, but I sure as hell am not going to let you kill the dog!"

"Listen Jess, if the owner comes forward, just tell them where the dog is. I will take the dog now," Liza said.

Liza said, "Between my dead ex-husband, my own struggle

with addiction, and a war in Afghanistan... Jess, yes, Charlie is screwed up."

Liza continued, "That is what life is about, living against the forces of our lives. Jess you do not have to be so damn angry, nor confront everyone. I get your point."

Lisa said, "Let us live our lives the best we can. Clean up the wreckage of our addiction. Jess, how about we try to heal those around us? I hope life heals Charlie. I hope life does bring him around. He has had more happen to him in his life, than should have happened to him in ten lifetimes."

Jess said, "Well you need to do something with him. He is outrageous and he is dangerous."

"Like I said, Jess," Liza replied, "Have him assessed. That is all we can do today. Now, if you will excuse me, I have a dog to take care of and a job to do."

CHAPTER 7: FINDING ROSIE

Looking back on John's memorial last month, Liza was not quite sure what had compelled her to go. Her husband, Gary, had said, "Do what you need to do." Gary trusted her to know best. She had flown to California looking to resolve her past. She needed to get things back in order and say goodbye to John, who was the father of her two children. Robert, her oldest son, had gone with her.

Robert was finishing college and had been accepted into law school. There were reasons that Charlie had not been able to go with them to his dad's memorial.

Emma had just been born.

Of course, Charlie did not want to leave Claire and Emma alone by flying off to California for his father's funeral. Claire and Liza both thought that was the right choice.

Liza had no idea that Johns' death would affect Charlie so much. Charlie's using had been spoiled by a Driving Under the Influence ticket last year, but damn it, he had been sober for a while. She thought he was better.

Liza was faced with getting structure and treatment arranged for Charlie again. This was not just her responsibility.

She had been hopeful that John would step up and do something. Now he was dead. He could not help anybody. Charlie and Claire had a new baby. What a mess!

How crazy was it for her to take on the dog? She was confused, because Charlie did not have a dog. Grabbing the dog by the collar, Liza walked right past the receptionist and into her office, closing the door behind her.

Turning loose of the dog, she sat in her chair and began to cry. "My God, how can I deal with all this?" she thought. "My son is destroying his life. His denial is so strong. In fact, he is unable to see clearly. Again."

As if on cue, Rosie nuzzled her head up against Liza's thigh. There she stood. Liza had not even realized Rosie was with her until that moment. She hugged Rosie and Rosie pushed back. "Where the hell did Charlie find you, Rosie?" Liza said as she scratched, behind her ears. "You are kind of a sweetie."

"I hope no one claims you, Rosie," Liza thought. "We need you." Liza petted Rosie on the head and rubbed her ears.

Rosie's calmness traveled to Liza.

In that moment she listened to herself take deep breaths.

Liza thought, "I do not want to violate the company rules. I do not want to violate professional ethics. I do not want to let my son down. I do not want Jess to treat Charlie like shit."

The tears just flowed.

The more she thought, the more she cried.

PART III: DEATH

CHAPTER 8: CHARLIE'S DEMONS

August 2011

Six weeks ago, I was headed south. A shouting match with Joe, my father-in-law, had led me to a hasty exit. The destination was my childhood home. After the barbecue, I had a beer. That one beer became an endless drunk. I had a long way to drive and not much to occupy my time.

Memories of his hometown and his childhood began to play in Charlie's head like a movie.

My fondest memories were of camping and swimming. My older brother Robert and I loved spending summers with Mom and Dad.

We loved fishing on the lake. Who could ever forget that boat? The boat was huge for two small boys. Robert and I would fish. Dad would help. Our dog, Zoey, was always at our side. That dog could swim, fetch, and receive our love.

In my crazy family, Zoey was a source of comfort and security. She ate, slept, and lived by my side. She was a trusted friend who never told a secret and was always happy to see me coming. Zoey was someone I could hug and hold and talk to.

I was in constant interaction with her. Zoey woke with me, ate with me, and slept in my bed at night. With a dog kiss, my life was easier to take.

Across that lake, you could see forever. When we were out there catching perch, it was simply one of the best things that ever happened for my brother and I.

We often went to Bone Creek Lake on weekends. Mom was always busy working or spending her time with friends, drugged up or shit-faced drunk. She worked the weekends as a waitress at a downtown café, working the breakfast shift until two in the afternoon.

That left my Dad in charge. He, too, was drunk most of the time. He would drink a case or two every weekend. Budweiser was Dad's number one priority. Driving home from the lake was tricky with a drunk. Robert would help. My big brother Robert knew the way, we always made the drive home safe. Robert became the parent as Dad slipped away into drunkenness.

The trauma of my life began pushing back in. I tried to think of happy memories. Most evenings were full of loud people, friends of my parents that came over. Mom and Dad would get high and stay up all night drinking with them. Zoey taught me how to be safe during dangerous nights.

Now, at age 26, here I am driving in a downpour on a stormy night. I can hardly see the road in front of me, and the windshield is cracked. The rain is coming down in solid sheets. I am heartbroken. I am angry. I am pissed.

Yeah, I kicked the car windshield out; I spidered the glass. I kicked hard enough to make the windshield split.

I was told I needed to get out of town. "We don't want your kind here," the officer said. "What kind is that?" I thought Maybe they thought I was on drugs? Nope, just drunk on whiskey this time.

The rain started to fall. A heavy shower and booming thunder and bright flashes of lightning. This lit up the whole night sky. Emotionally vacant, I tried to call Robert. No answer. I drove on.

Some son of a bitch honked at me. I yelled out loud, "Watch where you're going yourself, asshole!"

I cannot believe my wife Claire texted me, "Where are you?" the message, "I am worried."

"That bitch!" Charlie thought.

Charlie said, "Emma is not Joe's daughter, Emma is my daughter, damn it!"

Claire's father, Joe, is always butting in. He is sober. So he thinks he is better than me. I am so mad at Claire for kicking me out. The pounding rain on the windshield once again draws me out of my thoughts. What a hard, hard rain.

I lost my phone. Too bad, I would love to put this shit on Facebook Live. No one would believe such a downpour!

This highway is narrow. My headlights seem dim. A dark night drive. Pouring rain, I still have a long way to go.

I can get a cheap motel room in Louisburg.

A motel came in sight.

The place looked okay.

I pulled in then entered the lobby. The place smelled damp with its old dusty furniture and soiled, worn carpet.

Pressing the buzzer, the dull sound brought out a sleepy man to the lobby. With a critical eye he looked me over. The motel clerk said, "We don't want your kind here."

What? Did he really just say that? Twice in one hour.

I only had one beer, "Drugs?"

Well... I don't remember taking any.

I drew myself up to full height and spoke in a respectable manner.

"Can I have a room?"

From under the counter, the clerk pulled out a gun.

Looks like he might just have some experience getting rid of my kind.

"I am done. I am leaving," I assured him.

I put my hands up and my palms out to show him I meant no harm. I left.

I got back in my car and continued my journey north.

Damn, that gun was terrifying. All thoughts of a gun were quickly forgotten as the Oxycodone I had just taken started to kick in. Shit, was I ever high!

I was not in the wrong. I had done this before Emma was born and Claire knew that! She knew how much I liked to party.

Before we had Emma, she used to party with me! Kids do not stop people from getting high. My entire childhood is proof of that.

As I drove on, the pelting of rain on the car lulled me into memories of my childhood.

My Sweet Zoey, who always gave so unselfishly with her calm presence, kindness and loyalty.

I told Zoey once that I wanted to be a dog doctor. I spoke to her, believing she understood. That she wanted me to be a person people respected. I thought I was Zoey's protector and hero. The day she was killed, I found out I was only a vulnerable child.

In a world of drugs, drinking, neglect, and violence, Zoey was my closest friend. A deep bond of love joined us together.

That afternoon still fills me with absolute rage. The safety and security of having Zoey in my life was ended.

One night, when dad was in town from California, he had stopped by the house to see me and Robert. The visit started out fun with new toys. Then Mom and he started screaming at each other and fighting. On his way out Dad slammed the door. Revving his engine, he squealed his tires, signaling his departure. Then came the thud and a sickening high-pitched yelp, followed by lots of cussing.

I can remember running around the car to pick her up. My Zoey. She was crushed. My Dad had run completely over the center part of her body. There was no hope. She would die right there in my arms. As I held her warm body close to mine, I heard her breathing slow. I was not her hero; she was mine. I was not her protector; she was mine. "I am so sorry," is all I could say. Over and over, "I am so sorry."

I held her until my sobs dried up and she was cold. Mom put a mirror by her nose, "She is not breathing son."

"Where is dad," I asked. She said, "He left."

I asked, "Will anyone help me with my dog?"

Robert said he would.

A loud honk brought me back. Drunk alert!

I kept wishing Robert would call. I am so drunk. I lost my phone.

After Zoey died, things just changed. Those years were so

full of anger and endless arguments. It seemed like Mom and Dad never stopped fighting. Mom was mad all the time. Dad was gone all the time. He traveled to the West Coast a lot and then their divorce was final. He was never sober. I did not pay a lot of attention at the time. His trips away grew longer and longer, until I rarely saw him at all.

Lately, thoughts of my father seem to be constantly on my mind. Two months ago, the police had called Mom and broke the news that my dad was dead. It must have been a drug deal gone bad or an overdose. I do not really know. Mom is so tight-lipped about his death.

I wanted to fly out to California, but Mom and Claire both said no. Emma had just been born and Claire needed my help. I could not do anything for Dad anyway.

I miss him.

I knew that he sold drugs. I have heard Mom talk about those days. These last few months have been so difficult. I did not feel like I had anyone to turn to.

My brother, Robert, is still not answering his phone.

After my tour in Afghanistan, life just sucked. Everything started to spiral downward. Actually, I have a list of my pain, grief, and shame. I wrote the list when I was in outpatient treatment at the Veterans Hospital in Wichita. That treatment worked for awhile.

I had stopped the opioid drugs and the drinking before Claire became pregnant with Emma. Then I lost my father and the reoccurring dream of the lost child started again.

To numb that pain and deal with the grief, I started with just a few drinks. To those drinks I added opioids. That created more stress.

Having a newborn in the house added to the overwhelming feeling that I had lost control of my life. Claire became increasingly angry at me. Always yelling at me to help, until she eventually pulled away.

I felt so lost, hurt, alone, and confused. That is when my life took a real nosedive. The defining moment, one that I wish I could go back and do over. I hit Joe, my father-in-law.

With Claire retreating from my life and taking Emma with her, I began to focus on the U.S. president's instructions. A soldier on a mission waiting for orders. I am a trained Army Medic and my service to this country is highly respected. I have earned medals.

I started the opioids. I kept dreaming that evac. I just keep looking for that child over and over. I wake up and I just cannot find her under the soldier. That dream, that reoccurring dream, has no end.

The president had selected me to be part of the recovery mission. I am ready to go; just waiting on the call to duty. That is why there is a problem here. If I start the opioids again I will not be ready. I called them my whiskey days and opioid nights.

Honor

"A soldier is someone who, at one point in their life, wrote a blank check made payable to the United States of America for an amount up to and including their life." —Author Unknown

CHAPTER 9: SPIDER'S WEB

I t is morning on the first day in the Jackson County jail. The officer is taking me somewhere to think more clearly. Screw them!

In my mouth is the strong taste of vomit, and my head... my head feels like somebody's been using it for a basketball.

I feel awful.

I am having trouble thinking through exactly what the president wants me to do. Possibly work another disaster, like the Joplin, Missouri tornado a few months ago.

This time, I will try to make certain that County Emergency Medical Services bring more body bags. Wish I could forget. That level of destruction up close reminded me of a city fire-fight in Afghanistan.

There were over one hundred and sixty souls lost in the

Joplin tornado. My nerves are shot. The president has chosen me for another mission.

"No, I cannot eat," I told the officer, "I just threw up. Did you not hear me?"

"Did I mention my head feels awful? Like someone is bouncing it around. Oh my God, what happened last night anyway?"

My detoxification is worse than ever this time. "I dreamed I was holding Zoey." I woke up to a banging on the cell door of my detox room. The banging was so loud!

The officer shouted, "Stop screaming kid!" My clothes and entire body were soaked with sweat and I was curled up in a fetal position.

The officer asked me,"Why are you screaming?"

Cold and wet, I did not respond. My heart was thumping like it was going to jump straight out of my chest. I just laid there and did not respond.

That cruel death was replaying in my head.

The officer demanded, "Just shut up, kid, so I do not have to come back and check on you again."

Charlie said, "I am a veteran and I need medical care."

The officer reported, "We picked you up on a warrant. You are not going anywhere. You assaulted someone in Crawford County. Do you remember that? Do you remember who it was? The report says someone named Joe?"

Charlie sat there shaking.

The officer then said, "You got no choice from here, buddy. You will be transported to Crawford County Jail."

I cannot remember any of it. If I could, I would make something up to try to explain this.

I catch a glimpse of a memory. Did I crash my car? My memory is coming back to me now; lots of trash, and a broken car window. I need to just sit here until I figure this out. I remember the road. I remember the storm. I remember the car spinning and coming to a halt in a ditch. I was stuck and unable to move the car out of the ditch. Then Zoey appeared? Oh crap, Claire threw me out. Damn it, something had happened with her dad, Joe.

Did I hit him? Surely not! Joe is a jerk most of the time, but he is Claire's father.

"Charlie, the jail clerk wants to talk to you in about half an hour. Get yourself cleaned up and ready to roll," an officer tells me.

I feel so bad, I just want to die. They are going to do something with me and I do not even know what I did. Why am I not already released? Oh my God, what a mess!

I can barely move.

I have burned what Claire said was my last chance.

"Charlie, the jail clerk will see you now. You will have to stay cuffed until we do a final discharge," instructed the officer.

"Can you loosen these up a bit? My arms are still sore from last night. In fact, my whole body hurts."

"I am surprised you are even alive," the officer said.

"Mr. Charlie Redon, you were absolutely hammered last night. You were one obnoxious mess. Something will have to be done with you. You assaulted some guy in Pittsburg, Kansas."

No comment from me.

The jail clerk tells me that they will transfer me to secure detox at the jail in Crawford County and that there is a warrant out for my arrest on an assault charge. I am being charged with Driving Under the Influence that left my car in a ditch.

As I ask the clerk what happens next, I remember that the President has a mission for me. Informing the jail clerk of this does not seem to impress her like I had hoped it would.

The clerk moves her head to one side and asks, "The president?"

"Yeah, the President of the United States, I have a disaster recovery mission. I am waiting for my orders," Charlie said.

The clerk replied with a roll of her eyes, "We will have someone talk to you. I documented the mission down just like you told me word for word."

"Great," Charlie responded.

The clerk then said, "I think you need to be evaluated. I seriously would recommend getting off the stuff, kid."

"We are taking you to detox observation."

The officer cuffed me for the drive to Crawford County. It is never easy getting your head in a patrol car with your hands cuffed behind your back. I have bumped my head more times than I care to admit. Here I go, again.

I traveled with the officer for a couple hours. When we reached our destination, I realized I had been here before.

"Welcome back to the Crawford County jail detox Charlie," I whispered to myself. "Make yourself comfortable."

"This way to the intake room, Charlie. Sit right over here," said the Sheriffs Officer as he handed my paperwork to a booking clerk.

Sitting there, mentally preparing for the disaster recovery mission from the president, my imaginary military briefing begins.

The clerk reads from my file.

Charlie Redon

Charlie Redon, age 26, born November 21, 1984 in Pleasanton, Kansas. Mother, Liza Fitzgerald, Father, John Redon. Recovering alcoholic and addict previous treatments here listed.

Honorable discharge from United States Medical Services Corp, returned to hometown to work for Crawford County EMS after Afghanistan deployment.

Recipient of "Navy and Marine Corp, Afghanistan Campaign, Purple Heart Medals."

Subject reports first use of mood altering substance at around age 12 and continuing through time served as Army Medic.

Subject's mother is the Lead Counselor at the SEK Addiction Treatment Center in Southeast Kansas.

The subject has a family member, his uncle, working at the Sheriff's Department in Crawford County, Jess Redon.

Subject describes long history of alcohol and opioid abuse, intensifying after military service and the Joplin Tornado. First treatment episode was directly after military discharge from which he entered into recovery for two years, then relapsed after he worked emergency efforts in the Joplin Tornado, May 22nd, 2011. Subject reports the tornado caused him to experience flashbacks from the war, quote "too much destruction, too much death."

Subject reports that he and wife Claire were headed to Joplin that evening for dinner and shopping, then to attend an open AA meeting at St. John's Hospital. Subject reported, "We were driving in from the west around 5:30 p.m. I had taken care of Emma all morning so Claire could exercise with friends at the YMCA. It had been a perfect day for doing yard work at home in Pittsburg." Charlie said, "I had just finished up and showered when Claire reminded me she wanted to eat in Joplin and shop before we attended the open AA meeting at the St. John Hospital."

We were headed south on Highway 400 by Spring River Mental Health Center when the sky started to blacken. It turned an eerie color. I told Claire, "This doesn't look good. We are turning around and heading back home." We later learned that an E-F5 tornado had touched down at 5:34 pm, exactly 3 miles to the west of where we had turned around. That tornado was a mile wide and traveled 22 miles creating a huge path of destruction that killed one hundred sixty-one people.

```
Subject reported that as he pulled
back into Pittsburg, his County Emer-
gency Medical Services pager went
off. He spent the next 48 hours with a
search and rescue team that had been
organized for the four-state area in
an attempt to try to find, identify,
and manage all the destruction. Sub-
ject reports he identified and helped
with the removal of the deceased.

After this event, subject relapsed
into substance abuse and lost his
job at County EMS.
```

The intake clerk raised his head from reading the report and began to speak to Charlie. "What do you remember of the last two weeks, Charlie?"

I just sat there, dazed. My head felt three times its size. Everywhere I looked, it was like I had shaken my head five times and all I could see was confusion. So much confusion, on many different levels. Not the kind of confusion you experience when you are not remembering something, but more like the kind of confusion that comes when you are trying to figure out who is who. Was that nurse like Claire? Was that intake worker like my mom, Liza? Did the president put me here? To test me? Why? What disaster has hit now? Have I some type of involvement with another tornado again? Why are there gold flecks on the wall? Am I looking for treasure?

It just seemed like things were all wrong. I could not wrap my head around anything; could not seem to get it. So, I choose not to speak.

That officer, the intake guy, is acting just like Claire's dad, Joe.

"I relapsed big time, not sure what else I can say," I finally uttered in response to the intake worker's question.

Then he asked, "I see you received the Navy and Marine Corp Medal, for Army heroism in saving a life?"

Charlie just hung his head. "Yes"

Then in a whisper, "Well, the soldier was dead."

Charlie flashed back to that moment. With no word spoken, Charlie's mind and memory played tricks, like the music to a song you cannot get out of your head. The sound of helicopter rotors beat, the distinct smell and taste of dust mixed with helicopter fuel filled his nostrils, the vibration before the 'copter lift shook his chair. "I was on the rescue end of a fire fight in a small village north of the capitol. I had pulled two Marines out and was ready to load the Evac back, when I heard a dog bark above the flapping of rotors," thought Charlie.

"A small terrier mix — we nicknamed them "Rat Dogs" — was going nuts on a pile of rubble; just going ape. I heard her bark, but I saw nothing. Just a mangy dog. I ducked down and ran over to where the dog was and noticed a combat boot, barely visible beneath rock and rubble.

As I dug the soldier out, a small hand moved. The soldier had FALLEN ON A CHILD, saving her life. Silently Charlie pushed his memory for the name.

Charlie blurted, "Marine Corporal Michael B. Lee. He was the hero." About that, Charlie would speak no more.

Later, Charlie did ask, "Am I in a detox? You know I am in extreme physical pain and horribly confused. I think I fractured my leg."

The next day followed the same pattern. The nurse asked me questions and took my vital signs. The whole time I was in and out of a dazed confusion, dealing with incredible pain and a head smash.

"How are you today?" the nurse asked. I guess I must have looked at her too long without answering, because she did not even wait for my response.

I thought I just saw Jess. Wow, that is bad. My uncle Jess, Dad's brother. Or was it Jess? Maybe it was my dad, John. He is not really dead? Maybe he has something to do with the president's plan.

Finally Charlie muttered, "I am feeling pretty good."

"I keep dreaming that Evac. I just keep looking for that child over and over. I cannot find her under the soldier. Thank God the dog found her that day." Then, I wake up.

The nurse jerked her head around and looked intently at me, as if in shock that I was muttering.

"Glad to hear it," she said. "My name is Beth."

I asked her if my wife, Claire, had been in touch. Her response was, "Not to my knowledge. You have not been allowed any visitors."

"My wife is a nurse. Her name is Claire. We just had a baby; here is a picture of them. Sorry, the picture's waterstained"

"After you left Independence Police custody, you were sent to County Secure Detox," Beth explained, when I asked her where I was. She said, "You have been unable to speak much at all, and we were not certain about the extent of all your injuries. We knew about your leg injury, but the extent of your head injury was less straightforward. I will send in Don, your patient care navigator, and he will go over your intake information with you. He will make this as clear as he can."

Later that day, Don came in to take down all my details and he asked me question after question. He said that once my thinking cleared, I would be seeing Larry as my counselor and that Larry would define a strategy for my future care.

I do not know exactly when it happened, but a dog walked in.

A chocolate lab. Was this was the dog from my wreck? Zoey?

The intake worker asked, "Did you meet Rosie, the facility dog?"

My response was, "I'm still not sure." Yet, as soon as she entered the room, she came bounding towards me with lots of energy, determination, and love. I had myself a visitor, Rosie.

I called her name and she came and sat at my bedside. Don said, "Oh, I see you've met Rosie." Charlie hugged Rosie and said, "This is my angel that saved my life."

A while later, Larry came in. He was a short, stocky man with dark black hair and a gruff Italian accent. Larry expressed that he would be my counselor and that I would need to make some decisions after I detoxed. After he listened to my substance use and relapse history, I instantly felt the urge to say less. He seemed to think that I needed to say more.

"What do you recall about getting here?" Larry asked.

"I don't know," I responded. He assured me that once the fog cleared, the memories would come back.

Glad I am here? I am certainly not glad I am here. Not at all!

That chair over there looks comfortable. I think I am just going to sit. As I sat by the window looking out, I was wishing I was not here. I just wanted out of here. The only thing of interest that I can see is a damn spider's web. Here is the problem. I am not with Claire. I have lost her. I have relapsed.

And here is another problem. I am not with my child; my new little baby. My own flesh and blood. I am not with my child! No, I am here at this damn place. I need to leave. I am like that spider. No, I am not. I am like that moth that is caught in the spider's web and these people are the spiders!

Why will Claire not answer my texts, anyway? The waves of emotional hurt came rolling over me, only masked by my anger and resentment. I am such a mess. My life is destroyed. Done.

All I feel is pain. I am so hurt and just beyond depressed. What was I thinking? What was that shit about the president? Something about not accomplishing a mission? Man, I make no sense. I am so confused.

I look out the window past the spider and the moth, past me and my captured status. I see myself as the fluttering moth, in complete and absolute surrender. Through the window and into the other hallway, I see my father-in-law, Joe. Joe the man who pressed charges against me for assault.

How in the hell could this get any more complicated?

PART IV: HISTORY

CHAPTER 10: JUST FOR TODAY

The clock has now been turned backward almost a decade for Charlie's father-in-law, Joe. As the scene from the past played forward in his mind, Joe recalled how he had always thought of Charlie more like his own son, not just a son-in-law. Certainly not like this drunken asshole who had decked him right in front of his daughter, Claire.

Entry of Sergeant Joe in Skip's Journal:

I was sitting in a jail cell in Bourbon County, Kansas. My life was just about to take a major turn. Of course, at the time it felt like a turn for the worse. I felt like everyone was against me, even my own family. I had served my country. I had led men into battle to take ground, claiming those same hills over and over again in the jungles of Vietnam. We lost some damn good Marines. Most people do not think of death every day. I had to. Bringing my command home alive became my goal. My job was keeping people alive. The first casualty made winning that war personal for me. I was the baddest son-of-a-bitch in 'Nam. No fear allowed here.

Now, here I am in jail. Damn it, this is not my fault! That sucker was a smartass and had it coming.

My phone call today was with the VA (Veterans Affairs).

"First things first, soldier."

Who the hell called them? I felt like I was back in boot camp. Hell, I had to remind myself that I was retired. The VA official was rattling off my history like I don't remember all the fights and scrapes I've been in! He had talked to my family, and they all decided I needed to sit here until I chose an addiction treatment facility to go to. Do I want to go back to the VA Hospital or to a community-based primary care for addicts? That is the question. That answer is the only thing that will get me out of here, so I need to make a decision stat.

The VA official will not say which of my family members called him, the ass. It had to be my ex-wife, my girlfriend, or my daughter, Claire. Claire is just a child. Surely, none of the men that I consider brothers from my tours in 'Nam would have called them!

I told the guy where I thought a good facility might be; it had to do with his ass and a place where the sun does not shine.

So here I sit. Once again, I let my mouth overload my brain. Hope the food's good.

Fifteen days into my stay, Claire called. I have always had a soft spot for my daughter. She's beautiful, kind, gentle, and so incredibly smart. Well, she is my daughter.

She started in on me, "Daddy, what's going on? Mom says you're in jail for a fight in a bar?" Claire's mom is my ex-wife, Joyce.

"Daddy, get it together. Please! If you continue to destroy yourself, who is gonna be there for me? Don't you know that I need you? Who will teach me to drive? Who will come to my graduation? Who will walk me down the aisle when I get married? That is supposed to be you! Dad, I need you! Please, get help. Please, get better," Claire pleaded.

Of course I melted. I could never say no to my baby. I really wanted to be there for her. I needed to be there for her.

"When I was little, you were always there for me. You packed my lunch and fixed my hair. I don't need those things anymore, Dad, but I still need you. You were my hero then. Please be my hero now."

I sat there in jail, contemplating my life and Claire's words. Three weeks later, Ernie, my old Navy buddy, finally bailed me out. There with him stood Claire. My first thought was, "Now, we are talking. How about a beer?"

Nope, they had other ideas for me. Ernie had contacted Claire and together they had worked to get me into the Addiction Treatment Center in Girard.

They drove me straight there. Claire gave me the biggest hug at the entrance. She looked me directly in the eye and said, "I know you can do this, Dad. You can do this for yourself and for me. I have faith in you. You are my hero."

Ernie gave me a hard clap on the back and said, "Place the self-doubt in God's hands and tell the old enemy to get on out of here," ending with, "Just for today. Joe, stay here. Let go and let God take the lead."

CHAPTER 11: HIGHER POWER

Joe's Story

I start my story with entering the SEK Addiction Treatment Center. I would like to talk about my journey as a soldier and my recovery.

I was in the Addiction Treatment Center for thirty days. I attend this open meeting as a way to try and give back some of what I have received. Ten days after I got out of treatment, I found out I was going to be a new dad. I am 50 years old! I had been living with a lady 20 years younger than me who was not supposed to be able to get pregnant. Ten days after I got out of treatment, I found out she was pregnant.

I had a decision to make. Do I want to be a responsible person and take on being a father at 50 years old?

I do love this person. I decided to get married. I got out of treatment in November, and married in December.

⊚〜

Joe said, "A soldier who made friends with me in treatment called in January from Wichita, Kansas. He was experiencing a lot of medical problems. He wanted me to come see him. I had only known this guy for thirty days. I did not know if he just needed money or what the deal was. I took a chance and drove to Wichita."

Skippy was definitely telling me the truth. I saw him in the hospital. His liver and kidneys were shutting down. I visited him a few times in Wichita. His condition got progressively worse.

In February, at two in the morning, St. Francis Hospital called me. They asked me to identify myself, then informed me that my friend Skip had gone into surgery and died.

The last thing he did was sign a piece of paper. A paper that gave me legal right to his body, a Vietnam Service Medal, and a handwritten journal in the event that something happened to him.

It is my belief that a higher power entered my life through Skip's journal. Even though he was gone, Skip became my teacher in fellowship and recovery.

So I had not been out of treatment two months when I find out I am going to be a dad again. I had just gotten married. I have a dead body on my hands.

A dead body and a recovering addict's journal; a journal that is difficult for me to read. They are the handwritten words of a fellow soldier and friend.

The illness of addiction does not leave recovering addicts with much money, but we were able to obtain a lot in the Fort

Scott National Cemetery for Skippy.

My military buddy was cremated and we buried him. I called several people that were in treatment with us.

Peter, a friend of mine who was a pastor, held a small ceremony for Skip. We read some of his journal. Said our goodbyes.

With a heavy heart, I returned home. In life I have said my final goodbyes to many soldiers. Skip was special. In my last visit he was very much at peace. He said he had completed the fifth step of AA. He warned me not to be tricked by John Barleycorn. Then he laughed, "Oh I mean; do not get tricked again." Skippy had a big smile.

He perceived me, of all people, as his spiritual leader — his minister — and stated that he was honored by my visits. I told him that I could not find a bigger sinner, so I knew I had to come. We had held hands and recited the 23rd Psalm together.

We recited it just as a good as any recovering alcoholic who had not seen the inside of a church in decades could by memory. We talked at length about our spiritual program of AA, our reach for a high power and our desperate surrender. We were contemporary soldiers from the same war, united in a new battle together.

We said the Lord's Prayer, we hugged, then we said goodbye.

I was not prepared to do this again outside of war. I had read in the Big Book that we must "clean up the wreckage of our past."

Skip's journal was his wreckage, and as I read through it, I realized how little I really knew about him. I was learning how complex he was.

His wreckage was crystal clear to me.
Now, soldier to soldier, I read his story.

That wreckage began to sound like mine.
To my sincere joy, he wrote of his recovery from addiction.

From the Journal of Robert A., "Skippy"

> *Those who know do not tell, for in the telling, another's acknowledgment of their higher power might go unseen. We each, as addicts, must find for ourselves – in complete surrender – that power greater than ourselves. That power that whispers to us in our quiet moments of the path we must take as a Recovering Addict.*

> *An addict in recovery lives sober & substance free.*

> *An addict in recovery chooses their spot & higher power.*

> *An addict in recovery is grateful, seeing hope in total surrender.*

> *An addict in recovery acknowledges evil & recognizes the enemy.*

> *An addict in recovery forgives themselves & others.*

An addict in recovery embraces living & is always ready for action.

An addict in recovery waits.

An addict in recovery wants & expects nothing.

An addict in recovery knows his surroundings & interacts with purpose.

An addict in recovery is ready for change (for better or worse).

An addict in recovery can heal with a touch or with words.

An addict in recovery has witnessed their vision.

An addict in recovery can never lay down their tools or knowledge of recovery until death.

An addict in recovery knows the name on their soul.

Cleaning up the wreckage of my life became a pressing issue for me after reading through Skip's journal.

Skip had been prepared for this illness of substance abuse to progress.

Skip had left me a challenge, to raise the bar on the quality of my sobriety. That journal was his legacy.

I knew I had to accomplish my fourth and fifth steps. I have the opportunity to spread the AA message of, "How it

Works," Chapter 5 of the Big Book of AA.

July 26 of the following year, about nine months after I got out of treatment, Matt was born. Being a father is awesome. He is a great son. I was a dad again at the age of 51.

Matt was an infant in life. I was an infant in sobriety.

I started writing in Skip's journal.

Now the journal is mine, Skip had left it to me upon his death. A written opportunity ready to teach me, as a grateful recovering addict, to finish Skip's task of learning a higher purpose for my life. I am going to write to my newborn son the concepts of being in recovery.

Whether recovering or not any person can follow this path in daily life.

Skip's challenge was to follow his path in search of a higher purpose for a life.

I now entered the battlefield once again; this time addiction is the enemy.

The greatest battles are won in the mind.

CHAPTER 12: A PERSONAL CRISIS

Joe

T hose who do not recover are people who cannot or will not completely give themselves to this simple program, usually men and women who are constitutionally incapable of being honest with themselves," from the AA Big Book — Chapter 5

Sometime in September, which was about ten months post-treatment, my wife found a lump on the right side of her neck. She saw the doctor and he wanted to perform a biopsy. Within a week of having the procedure, my wife was diagnosed with metastatic melanoma, stage three.

Joe said, "We have a two-month-old baby. I'm not even ten months out of treatment."

Thank God for the oncologist in Pittsburg, Kansas who recommended that we go to Mayo Clinic in Rochester.

With the help of my in-laws who had a fifth wheel, we loaded up our two-month-old baby, and headed out to face this very serious situation.

We clung to each other emotionally and spiritually. I brought my big AA book along, my 12-step book, my Little Red Book, my Bible, and Skip's journal.

My newborn son and I were both in our infancy. He in life and I in recovery.

My wife and I were stuck somewhere between total shock and complete surrender. We were struggling with limited knowledge and were totally, absolutely vulnerable.

Our higher power was all we had to rely on. I could either sedate myself by getting drunk; or I could work the Alcohol Anonymous program and write in Skip's Journal.

If I chose the AA program, I could see my total surrender and spiritual growth as I wrote in the journal.

We were in Rochester for two months, during which time my wife had surgery. In November, we came home.

They did not recommend chemotherapy or radiation.

She participated in a trial treatment which involved Interferon.

In January, I worked midnight to eight and while I worked, my mom and dad watched our new baby, Matt.

For the next 12 months, I was the one that gave my wife, Cathy, her Interferon shots three times a week. They made her deathly ill. Somehow, we managed to survive.

After her treatments, she was tested again. They found no signs of cancer.

In April, she went in for another scan. This time they found a golf-ball-sized tumor in her abdomen.

Back to Rochester we went. They determined that it was contained. Surgery could be performed in either Rochester or back at home. Via Christi removed the cancer at home.

As I sat in the doctor's offices and hospitals praying for my wife's recovery, Skip's journal was always at hand, always available to read and write in.

"Let go and let God," was my neverending companion.

My Navy buddy had been so right. Since the day that I was released from jail, I have been sober. I am still sober day by day.

When talking to fellow addicts, like my son-in-law, Charlie, about recovery and emotional triggers that are a part of re-lapse, I sometimes tell my own story.

I do not believe Charlie has any reason to go out and use, because an addict cannot afford to lay down his principles of recovery.

Learning to remain sober as a Recovering Addict must be put to action. The journal is about action.

Daily life is not just shits and giggles. You will experience life's good and bad events as a person. Being in recovery by surrender, teaches how to live as a warrior on life's terms.

"God will save your soul and AA will save your ass," that's what Skip wrote.

My journal gave this old soldier a place to see my trail of sobriety in words.

Skip taught me some necessary actions for recovery.

My wife and I have made numerous trips to Mayo's and KU Med and each time that well-worn Big Book of AA and Skip's and now my journal are right by my side. That journal has become our mutual path for recovery.

In all my recovery to date, over ten years now, I have received thousands of grateful gifts for being clean and sober.

Out of all of them, I consider two of those gifts to be my greatest. I was able to support my wife through her cancer diagnosis and treatment. Clean and sober.

When my father passed away, I was also able to support my mother. These are the gifts I would not trade for anything. The process of getting to this point in my life has been challenging and painful. A trail I walked clean and sober.

In a way, so was Skip, and all the other AA members in fellowship who were following a path of recovery.

"Rarely have we seen a person fail who has thoroughly followed our path." Big Book of AA, Chapter 5. "Those who do not recover seem to be incapable of being honest with themselves."

In order to win the greatest battles, that is what recovery has to be, amidst the forces of their lives. A grateful addict in recovery embraces life and sees hope. I was there, clean and sober, and I was able to participate.

I love my life and I love my family. Not all of my life has been pleasant, far from it. I consider that a gift as well, right along with Skip's death. His body just could not hold up any longer. His liver and kidneys simply gave out.

Following the path of recovery, with him in mind, keeps me connected. Skip keeps recovery real for me.

We know we are sober today, and we know that if we relapse there's no guarantee that we will ever return.

Skip did not return. I believe that when you are in recovery, you can never remove yourself from the reality of the world of addiction.

That battle just never ends.

As described by Skippy in his journal:

> *A Warrior lives sober and substance free. In doing so, he stands ready to battle the forces of his life in the here and now, unwilling to waste his life as I have. I am dying of liver failure.*

PART V: CHILDREN

CHAPTER 13: IN THE MIDST

Claire

Growing up, my father Joe was very strict. I do not remember having much of a childhood. I saw my friends having fun. I remember always having to be very responsible and mature.

I always struggled to just remember all of the rules.

As a teenager, I rebelled. I was a walking contradiction. I got A's, was a star of the volleyball team and softball team, and cheerleader. I joined every club. Every weekend I was drinking heavy.

I did carry the family pride. People perceived me as together, smart, and capable.

Ten years ago, I confronted my Dad regarding his drinking.

Liza says I was the family hero. I think that's good. If not good, then at least meaningful.

Meaningful in that it is Liza's job to understand the dynamics of addiction and recovery in families.

Living in this family is a more intense story.

My outer shell of aloofness was hiding a very vulnerable adult child.

I think Emma's grandmother, Liza, knows this.

She seems to understand me very well, possibly better than I even understand myself. Life has taught her a lot.

Once again, Liza and I are hugging and hoping that her son, my husband, Charlie, will mentally return to us and work a sobriety path in order to save his life.

In a way, our paths together were understandable.

Charlie's home was chaotic with little structure. Mine was the opposite. I was now rebelling against anything and everything; partying, drinking, and breaking all the rules.

Anything that I was not supposed to do, I did. I met Charlie, at a party.

He was so much fun. He offered me a break from the stress of my life. I loved it.

My parents put so much pressure on me. They wanted me to have a better life. To be perfect is stressful.

Drinking gave me a freedom that I did not have in other areas of my life.

I felt so free when I drank. Every single weekend I tried to drink. A break from all the pressures in my life.

Charlie was just an added bonus. We could drink together and have fun.

I felt safe and accepted unconditionally with Charlie . He was just simply a nice guy.

Our relationship quickly accelerated. Wild and reckless, we clung together.

I managed to make it through high school, partying every weekend. I even graduated with honors in my class.

Charlie headed out for military time. I went to college. In college I gained more independence and personal freedom and my need to use alcohol lessened.

Charlie was a different story. During and after his military service, his need for alcohol increased.

Charlie soldiered in the Afghanistan War as an enlisted Army Medic. The experiences he was faced with there accelerated his drinking behavior.

We began growing apart as his drinking and using began to increase.

I was focused on my college degree and nursing. Charlie's interest was what substance he could use and abuse next.

The worst part was he had no insight.

Liza finally intervened and confronted Charlie, placing him in a military recovery program. I believe that only served to spoil his drinking. Charlie had no deep recovery commitment.

We were on the verge of separation. One little test changed everything. I was pregnant.

We discussed and debated what to do. The result was for us to get married.

During that period of time, Charlie had completed his first round of treatment. He was stable and sober. I knew that our life would never be the same, but with Charlie sober it appeared that we at least had something to build on.

Charlie did not disappoint. While I was pregnant and even after Emma was born, Charlie was amazing. He worked hard to stay sober. He helped around the house, and promised to be the dad he never had.

A warrior is ready for change (for better or worse).

On May 22, 2011, our lives were interrupted by the Joplin tornado. Charlie worked that disaster as a first responder. He witnessed massive death and destruction. As I look back, I can clearly see the post-traumatic stress that started creeping into his life. Then it creeped into our lives.

My first priority was taking care of myself and our unborn child.

As a first responder, Charlie was simply performing the duties of his job, but witnessing all that devastation was taking an extreme toll on him. First, on his sleeping patterns. Later, on his daily thinking.

He began to self-medicate with alcohol in order to deal with the nightmares and tormenting thoughts during the day. He needed to see a therapist.

The reoccurring intrusive thoughts began to intensify, as he started reliving his military deployment. He could not sleep. His drug of choice evolved to Oxycontin, the same drug he had used when injured in Afghanistan.

A huge problem. Opioids and alcohol were not a good plan.

He was hiding his behavior from his mom. Then, his dad died.

When John died, Emma had just been born. I did not want to be left alone while Charlie traveled to attend his father's memorial.

Hindsight is 20/20 and that was possibly a bad choice on my part.

In all fairness, Charlie's dad John was not a good man. He

was an even worse father. John was a selfish addict and a drug dealer. It was to everyone's relief that he had continued his disastrous living far away in California.

These statements do not belong solely to me. These are things that I have heard said by Charlie's own family, his Uncle Jess and his mom Liza.

Charlie took his father's death hard. The self-medicating was not working. There was no good result from the substances he tried. His fragile recovery was gone.

Liza told me that in her heart, she knew the outpatient military addiction treatment had only spoiled the using, not stopped it. "A head full of AA and a belly full of booze don't mix, it ruins your drinking."

Liza said, "The first three steps of AA have just not come alive for Charlie. He is weak. He is lost. He has no path."

"She lost me with that one," Claire thought "I totally do not understand. If I had not confronted my dad Joe when he was in jail, he would still be drunk today. Seriously, it is that simple. End of story."

Gradually, the appearance and obviousness of Charlie's substance abuse became all too real.

Confronting it was put on hold though, as I gave birth to our child. I later became very concerned for the safety of Emma and myself.

After consulting with Dad and Charlie's mom, I decided I needed to work an Al-Anon program and declare myself powerless over his addiction.

Emma's arrival was the third and final trigger. There was the tornado, John's death, and a new baby. Everything changed when Emma arrived. I had a deep, vulnerable feeling for my child. A desire for her to have all the best in life.

Those early days after Emma's birth were a long, hard blur.

Just weeks after Emma was born, Charlie fell right back into his old habits.

I did not fully understand his addiction. I just felt abandoned by him. I gained some clarity after speaking with Liza and I began to better understand the progression of this disease.

One day, I had finally had enough. We had so many fights so many times, over and over, but nothing ever changed.

So I left.

I talked to my dad about our problems. I packed our stuff, grabbed Emma and moved in with Dad. I had just taken a huge first step towards changing our lives for the better. So I thought. Actually, that is when things really ignited.

Charlie came to my dad's house and confronted him. It got physical.

Dad called the Sheriff's department and reported the assault. Charlie jumped in his car and sped away. It was over four weeks later that I finally got any news about Charlie. He was in police custody and believed he was on a mission from the president.

By that point, I was too exhausted to care.

CHAPTER 14: I HAVE TO SEE CHARLIE

ergeant Joe was not one for small talk. His time in jail along with his physical deterioration had brought him to believe in the first step of AA. Now it was Charlie's turn to listen. Joe struggled to recognize his "too angry" attitude and forced himself to spend a moment in silence to get in touch with some serenity. His phone rang, abruptly interrupting his meditation.

In that moment, Joe came to the understanding that God was doing for him what he could not do for himself. Ten years ago his daughter, Claire, had forced him into treatment. She had saved his life.

Joe spent his entire military career trying to do just that... save people's lives. He was now faced with trying to do the same for his son-in-law. Charlie had a direct path to certain death. What could he possibly do or say to save him?

Joe answered the phone. First he heard shortness of breath. Then came the sobbing and broken speech, followed by a palpable emotional outburst. It was difficult to make out the words. Was it Claire?

"Sweetie, where are you?" Joe asked.

Pausing to catch her breath, Claire replied, "At your house, on the front steps."

Her tears and disappointment carried through the phone in her words. The story she told could have been Joe's own confessional.

He was reminded of his own bad behavior, faults and shameful misgivings, and his hard life lessons with Claire's mother.

As she spoke, he wondered if she realized who she was talking too. She was too upset.

Joe was struck silent as he listened to his daughter's story that so closely resembled his own.

A paralleled retelling of what he had done over the years. This was not his story, it was Charlie's story. This was the story of a wife of an addict, and the depth of her pain was heartwrenching.

Claire had saved his life and it seemed to him that trying to comfort her right now with a simple, "Let go and Let God," just somehow was not enough.

Slogans, sayings, and any spoken word seemed too trite for the daughter he loved dearly, the daughter who had thrown a ladder down a deep dark hole when he was in a pit of despair and surrender.

His daughter had saved his life. He had thought that no one cared. His daughter had met him in his darkness and helped him face his addiction. How could he do anything less for her?

"I will go see Charlie, yes. I will go to talk to him, Claire. Listen, sweetie, we just have to take this one day at a time. I know it is super painful and I know that you want to fix this, but we are going to have to be patient and get through this day by day," Joe reassured Claire.

To himself, all Joe could think about was how he wanted to kick Charlie's ass, the little prick.

"I am not going to allow him to treat my daughter this way."

Joe knew, both intellectually and in his heart, that Charlie had a progressive disease. He also knew that kicking his ass would not help anything. "I need to calm down," Joe thought. "I need more patience. I need something, but God, I have no clue what it is!" He needed to calm down before he talked to Charlie or he would strangle him! He had so much rage.

Joe pulled out the journal and flipped through entries. He read some of what both he and Skip had written. He stopped when he got to the trail for recovering addicts. As he read through Skippy's list and thought of the items he had tweaked and the ones he had created himself, Joe had an idea. We are (Warriors). We are all Warriors!

Skippy, Charlie, and I are all soldiers! I will go through this journal and write in an effort to touch Charlie's pride and honor.

Joe read aloud what he would give to Charlie.

Those who know do not tell, for in the telling, another's acknowledgment of their higher power might go unseen. We are Warriors in Recovery. We must find for ourselves — in complete surrender — that power greater than ourselves. It is that power that whispers to us in our quiet moments, showing us the trail we must take as Warriors in Recovery. In the world of addiction, this is a Trail of the Warrior.

A Warrior lives sober and substance free.

A Warrior chooses their spot and higher power.

A Warrior is grateful, seeing hope in total surrender.

A Warrior acknowledges evil and recognizes the enemy.

A Warrior in recovery forgives themselves and others.

A Warrior embraces living and is always ready for action.

A Warrior waits.

A Warrior wants and expects nothing.

A Warrior knows his surroundings and interacts with purpose.

A Warrior is ready for change (for better or worse).

A Warrior can heal with a touch or with words.

A Warrior has witnessed their vision.

A Warrior can never lay down their tools or knowledge of recovery until death.

A Warrior knows the name on their soul.

In that moment, Joe knew what he could do. He would go by the jail and try to see Charlie. He would either get in to see Charlie or he would not. He could leave a journal for Charlie. He could give Charlie something to read and write in. Maybe Charlie would read the journal that Skippy and he had created. Just as Skippy had stimulated Joe's thoughts in recovery, Joe hoped that he could also stimulate Charlie to take action.

Had Charlie's life become unmanageable enough? Without honest surrender, there was no way Charlie would hold onto his recovery. He had to start somewhere. He had to find and believe in a power greater than himself. Joe picked up the journal and headed to the jail. As he turned into the parking lot, he thought, "I need to add one last item to this journal."

"If pride and memory have a fight, pride always wins."

With that thought, Joe began writing from his heart. He penned one more entry into that new beloved journal.

From the Journal of Robert A. "Skippy," & Joe

Dear Charlie,

As addicts in recovery, when our lives become unmanageable, we must seek a higher power. This is where we truly experience and gain our strength in recovery. Your higher power might be a tree or a dog, Rosie. It might be Jesus, or even God as you understand him. We simply start somewhere and connect on a day-by-day basis, and that is how our ability will grow. That higher power will begin to teach us what it means to be sober. From there, we tune in and listen each day as we journey through the steps of AA in fellowship with other recovering addicts. With that being said, it is obvious to me that your life has become unmanageable. My proposal to you is that you give thought to the idea that maybe a power greater than yourself can help restore you to sanity. If you can't understand this fully today, please just follow the trail of the warrior and the 12 steps of AA.

As Joe turned the car into the jail parking lot, he felt a huge wave of determination rush over him. This was different than what he had ever faced in Vietnam. How would Charlie go about winning this battle? What would the outcome be?

He could not let his daughter down. He just could not let Claire down. Even though he did not know what to do next for Charlie he still felt the sting from Charlie's fist. He had to dig down deep. Look at Charlie as a person; a person with an illness, a person in desperate need of recovery, and a person whose life was being wasted.

Regardless of how he felt about Charlie's actions, he needed to see Charlie as someone with a disease that had progressed. Progressed to the point that the most important people in Joe's life were being affected. Joe's daughter and her child, Emma.

Joe felt his anger bubbling to the surface again as he thought, I am not putting up with that shit from that dumbass kid. Immediately he realized that there was no value whatsoever in his resentment, but damn, it sure felt good to mutter it to himself.

That's all he was doing, muttering it to himself. He was not saying it out loud, "I will kill that bastard if he harms my daughter, and I will kill him twice if he hurts my grand-daughter, Emma. I will protect them both," he continued mumbling to himself.

There is no valor in harming someone with a disease.

For a moment, as Joe sat there in the parking lot, he flashed all the way back 10 years ago to the death of Skippy, and to his journal. The journal of misshaped statements and confusing writings. The journal that Joe had struggled through as he wrote and rewrote, thought, prayed, and struggled over in an attempt to keep himself sober and clean all these years.

Deep emotions came over him as he thought maybe, just maybe, this is what it is all about.

I will do my best to set aside my rules and demands on that little punk. I will try to just go in there and treat him with the respect a solider deserves. Joe mumbled to himself, "Can you try not to be such an idiot, Charlie? You have a brand new baby!"

The last time I saw Charlie a big argument ensued. He was drunk and acting crazy and I just wanted to smash him.

Claire told me not to. I left that night and went home, thinking, "I am sorry your worthless dad is dead. He was not bringing you any value though, not while he was using." Then, I thanked God for the end of another day. I had another day sober.

Joe knew almost immediately upon entering the jail that he would not be able to see Charlie. As he sat there in the lobby, with the journal in his lap, he spent a moment in silence contemplating. What was he thinking? No one would give him access to see Charlie. What was he doing here wasting his time? Still, there he sat.

Determined to try anyway, Joe pushed the button and the matron asked, "Can I help you?"

"Joe Hanks, I'm here to see Charlie Redon."

"One moment please, let me check. Are you family?"

"I'm his father-in-law. He is married to my daughter Claire."

"The Deputy told me to tell you that Charlie's in seclusion right now. He is in the padded detox cell."

Joe said, "I told my daughter that I would see him. Is it possible that I could step inside?"

"I will ask the Deputy. Give me one moment please."

"The deputy says that is all you can do just step inside, until he either comes down, or stops acting so crazy. He is simply not safe. So, you can see him through the observation glass, but that is all you can do."

Joe's glance lingered on Charlie and he heard the electronic door slide open and out came Deputy Jess Redon, Charlie's uncle. Jess and Joe knew each other; they were more contemporary than some of the young guys.

Without thinking, Joe said, "I brought this for my son-in-law. Can you make certain he gets it?"

"Sure, I'll give it to him," answered Jess, "Joe, we only got him here because you filed the assault charge. That is the bench warrant they picked him up on with his dog."

Joe said, "Jess, that was my tough love, I was trying to get Charlie to understand that his actions have consequences."

Jess said, "Joe, you look terrible."

Joe replied "I ain't gonna lie, It's been hard. I have been watching my daughter's family fall apart. My granddaughter deserves a better life than this."

"Tell me about it," Jess said. "His father, my brother, John, certainly wasted his life. I would sure like to see Charlie step up."

"We are all family, no doubt about that," Joe said. "I just wish we were all a recovering family."

"Ya," Jess snapped. "I will make sure Charlie's gets the journal."

With that, Jess abruptly turned and walked away.

Taking out his phone, Joe called Claire and left her a message. Joe detailed his visit, "Claire, I thought I would give you a call back. I went to the jail and I saw Charlie. That is all I can say really. Charlie's in a bad spot. He looks like he has been beaten. He may have some fractured bones. Jess showed me a picture of your car windshield. It is definitely a total wreck. There is nothing more that can be done for Charlie at this point. Charlie is still coming down. We're just going to have to wait a few more days, possibly weeks."

"We don't know when someone will fall off. Everyone has another relapse in them, even me. Thank God that for today, I am ok. Even though everyone has another relapse in them, not everyone has another recovery in them. We'll just have to see how Charlie comes out of this. We'll just have to keep trudging this road to recovery with him.

"Claire, you really need to go to an Al-Anon meeting. I'll watch Emma for you. Just go to a meeting; this will take a while and will be a long process. By the way, when did you all get a dog? Jess mentioned something about a dog. They actually arrested Charlie with this dog in a gas station, after Charlie ditched his car."

CHAPTER 15: LIVING CHILD ABUSE

Jess' visit with Charlie

The door flew open to the detox room. Charlie looked up. Jess stood there, blocking the entire doorway. Charlie cowered in the corner.

"I talked to your mom, Chaz," said Jess. Charlie's dad had called him "Chaz" when he was in grade school.

At that moment all Charlie could see right now were Jess' fists. They were doubled up and clenched at his sides, as if they were made solely for hurting people. From his position in the corner, Charlie was eye-level with those fists. As Charlie looked up, it was his dad that he saw. He heard and felt his presence. His vision focused on those fists. Charlie knew from childhood experience that those fists were capable of inflicting a whole lot of pain. Physical and emotional terror ran through him, as he cringed and softly whispered,

"Dad?" Charlie's legs went weak. Charlie slid down the wall to the floor.

Jess, not thinking of his resemblance to his brother, John, stood ready to defend himself. Jess was braced for a physical confrontation. If this drugged, crazed man jumped, Jess wanted to be on guard.

All Charlie could think about was his dad. As a child, he had suffered so much abuse at his father's hand. Charlie shook his head a few times hoping to see reality a little more clearly.

Jess studied Charlie, trying hard to fight the emotions. Jess felt guilt and pity for his nephew, Charlie. Jess thought of the days when John had returned from Vietnam. John had been so wild. The entire family had asked Jess to intervene. Jess had failed to fix John.

How could something so destructive travel from father to son? It pissed Jess off to even look at Charlie. Charlie brought back all the memories of John's incessant and ridiculous demands. Seeing him now Jess wondered, "How did that little nephew Chaz ever make it through the Afghanistan War, with a medal no less?" "I love that boy." Jess had not meant to say it out loud, but he did.

Jess noticed the bruises on Charlie's hands and face. Sadness crept in. Jess was sad for Charlie. Sad for the little boy who was not okay, the boy who was an absolute mess. Those compassionate sentiments did not last long.

Jess threw Joe's journal on the floor near Charlie. Mission accomplished. Jess had done what Joe had asked him to do.

Charlie did not remember Jess' visit. He sat on the floor feeling vacant and numb, thinking he had been visited by his father, yet his father was dead? As Charlie's withdrawal from drugs continued, his fragile grip on reality was threatened. He was betrayed by his emotions of guilt for not attending his dad's funeral. In Charlie's psychotic mind, his Dad had been present. Flooded with grief, Charlie lay frightened. Only time and detoxification could help the psychosis that was currently in his brain.

Charlie's shouted as his anxiety rose, "I have to."

Jess closed the detox door.

As Jess walked away to the booking office his cell phone rang.

"Jess, it's Robert. I did not know who else to call. Uncle Jess, did they find my brother?"

Jess replied, "Yes, he is here in detox. Again."

"Charlie called me and I could tell it was bad," said Robert "He was most likely in a black out. When he is really drunk, his emotions are on the surface and he talks more about Dad and Zoey."

CHAPTER 16

John Barleycorn & Rosie

y phone tells me it has been twenty-four days since my last text from Claire.

Charlie is about completed with detox and is on the edge of deciding whether he will stay for substance abuse treatment or leave. He hopes that he reaches Claire.

Charlie texts Claire again, "Can we talk?"

Claire does not respond, so Charlie calls because he wants to hear her voice, even if he just gets her voicemail. As if sitting before a priest at confessional, Charlie starts imposing himself upon the unsuspecting answering recorder with a sad rant.

"I thought I could have just one beer; big mistake. The whiskey made me feel better. It made me feel less alone. Dad is gone, Claire. John is dead!

"Look, I started toward Ottawa, hoping to check out my old hometown ghosts and put them to rest. One thing led to another and then I ended up in a ditch near Kansas City, Missouri. I spent the night in a gas station, in the city of Independence, in the pouring rain. Then I was arrested. I am so sorry. Please give me another chance, Claire? I woke up in detox with a memory that gives me hope. Please come visit me. I am supposed to go talk to an Intake Worker at the Addiction Treatment Center now. Guess I am stuck here for a while. I love you. Bye."

After the phone call Charlie went to his therapy session. His intake worker listened as Charlie began telling what happened.

I can remember coming from Liza's house Friday night, really drunk. Mom confronted me, asking me if I had been drinking. I remember telling her, I sure hope not! I left in a hurry to get home. I laid there with the bed swirling around me, when I realized it was not my home anymore! Claire had kicked me out! I was so pissed that I got up and started right in on the whiskey. That's it. That's all I can remember from the last four weeks, because I blacked out, and ended up in jail.

The more I thought about Dad's death, the more I resented him. How had I ever expected to be a decent father, when I never had one of my own? I thought I could drink one beer just to relax and think. That one beer turned into one more and one more... I became more and more upset and my remedy was to keep drinking. Drinking and taking pain medicine in order to feel better, that's what I did."

Charlie started to tear up. "I'm already at the point where I just cannot see myself sober, not drinking or using."

Tears rolled down Charlie's face as he continued, "It really started eight weeks ago. I did the exact same thing with Claire. I had been able to keep it hidden from Mom. That did not work with Claire at all. An argument quickly led into a shouting match with Claire yelling at me to get out.

I tried to call my brother, Robert, but he did not answer. I knew my mom would be on Claire's side, so I just waited it out. A week went by and, for a while, I was okay.

Then all the resentments crept back in, a deep anger. I felt the need for a beer, to calm myself. I was searching for some comfort, which never arrived.

It baffles me that I am back in jail again. I really thought I would be fine. John Barleycorn is so seductive.

As I am telling my story, depression over my Dad is just so strong that I wish I was dead. How am I not dead? The way my car spun into that ditch full of water, and the water pouring in through the cracked windshield. That should have drowned me.

If I was dead, it would all stop.

If not physically dead, then at least dead to this deep rage and endless shame."

I was driving, wasted, and my mind started traveling through all of my life problems. Like when Claire walked out and took our Emma.

What that said to Charlie without words was, "Shame on you. You are a terrible father."

I would guess you therapy people would call that my trigger. I was left alone. It was just me and Jack Daniels.

ALL I wanted was to talk to Claire, then Joe came home. Claire's father's is a recovering addict who thinks he's a better dad than I am.

I just pushed him to the side so I could get the hell away from him, then he went and pressed assault charges against me.

The intake worker responded with, "Are you sure there was not more to the assault?"

 Charlie replied, "With Claire and Emma gone, I felt like I did not have anything left to live for. The resentment and the anger were all self-consuming. I kept thinking about my dad."

On my drive, I was brought back to reality when I saw those glaring headlights and heard the blare of that horn. I quickly swerved back into my own lane.

 I was hungry and so tired. I knew I needed to find a place to sleep. I struggled to read the road signs, as I drove towards the bright lights of the city, the rain glaring off the cracked windshield. All the road exchanges were confusing.

 Lost and tired, I just wanted to find a quick place to stop. I took that clover leaf thinking I would get gas and food and clear my head.

 When I turned the wheel to take that exit I just kept going

and going, around and around in a circle.

The car went sliding out of control in the rain. It was spinning all over that clover leaf. I thought it would never stop.

As the car continued spinning, I felt a fluttering around my head. Spinning and turning, the car finally came to a stop with a loud thud and that is when the cracked windshield gave way, and all that water burst in.

The protective fluttering around my head continued while the car began to sink. That is when I realized I was going to die. The thought flashed in my head, I am dead.

Out of the black darkness, I noticed, the outline of a large animal swimming toward me.

As suddenly as dread had come, the dread left and was replaced by a profound sense of peace. I found footing in the water. Eventually I was able to just follow the animal back to shore. The animal was a Labrador dog.

Had I known what was going to happen next, I surely would have paid more attention.

I felt a sense of peace, like a cool chilled rain.

I looked, I saw, I hugged my warm angel. I hugged her tight to me as I then replayed the accident over in my head.

"The Big Book promises that our God will do for us when we can not do for ourselves."

The dog's name tag read Rosie, but in my heart the tag read Zoey. My own personal angel, sent back to keep me safe. Zoey, my guardian, my protector and hero. Her death still haunted my childhood memories.

Looking around, I saw the lights of the gas station and I started walking towards them. Out of the black cold rain, I walked with my childhood dog Zoey at my side. What a beautiful chocolate lab she was.

Manny, the gas station clerk, was shouting to get my attention, I asked him to help me get my car out of the ditch, but he said he could not right now. Maybe in the morning. He must have thought that I needed to sit there and rest. There we were, just the dog and me. Hungry, tired, and alone. No wait, not alone, we had each other.

In the back of my mind, I know that when my car started to turn, I was in a place of surrender.

I let go of the wheel because I had no control as the car spun and turned, ultimately landing in the ditch.

I know I surrendered in that very moment.

I had lost control of not only my car, but my entire life. My whole life was one huge mess. I was a huge mess.

Thank God the gas station attendant refused to help me get my car out that night, because I would be dead.

Thank God they recognized what I could not... that I was at my end. I was saved by Rosie and Manny. They saved me! Seems so unreal now.

The intake worker began to speak. "According to the police report, Charlie, the gas station clerk thought you were on drugs and called the police. There is a description of you walking up to each semi-truck in the parking lot, making the sign of a cross on each one. One by one, as if you were blessing them.

"They reported that you did this for an hour and a half, to every semi in the lot. That is over 30 trucks. Charlie. I have spoken with the officer on duty that night and read the police report. Let me read to you from the transcript, which starts with a phone call to the Independence Police Department.

"Quote, this is Manny at the QuickTrip Truck Stop at the Junction of 470 & I-70, north of town. Is Officer Kelley on duty this morning? Could you ask him to swing by for his morning coffee? I have something I need him to take a look at."

Officer Kelley relayed in his report and direct quotes from the attendant, "It's the dangest thing I ever saw. It was like a wall of water coming down, it was hitting so hard, Officer Kelley. Out of the rain, here comes this soaking wet man and a dog. Both just dripping wet and throwing water to and fro. I wanted to tell them both to get back outside, that's what I wanted to do.

"The dog was shaking and throwing water everywhere, then the guy starts hugging the dog and just wouldn't let go. I have never seen anything like it.

"This guy was hanging onto this dog, like it was his lifeline.

"Like he thought without the dog, he was a goner.

"No, wait a second, listen to the rest of this. The wall of

water finally comes to a halt and the dog laid down. The guy got up and walked outside. See those diesel out there? There were thirty of them at the time.

"He walked to the front of each of those trucks and crossed it like he was a priest or something. I watched him do it. I was afraid he might hurt somebody or himself.

"Seriously, he crossed every one like a priest, then he turned around and walked back over here and laid down by his dog."

Ever so quietly Manny said, "Wait until you see him with that dog. When I saw your car coming, I told him to get in the bathroom and clean up. Just wait."

Charlie came out of the restroom and said, "My name's Charlie. What did you say your name was?"

"Officer Kelley."

"And you want to see my ID?"

"Yes."

"It's wet, but it's right here."

"Charlie, I see you live south of here. What brings you this way?"

"I was traveling home, sir."

"I see that you're not driving now. Was anyone with you?"

"No, sir. I was alone. Oh wait, I had my dog with me. My dog, Rosie."

"Ok, and where are you and Rosie headed to now?"

"We're headed south, Officer. I've had some problems and I was just headed south, trying to get them sorted out in my head."

"Is that your car in the ditch that I saw as I came around the clover leaf?"

"Yes sir."

So there I was, talking to an officer about what happened and him asking me about the dog and the wreck, about the water filled ditch and the broken windshield, about my car which was now completely submerged.

Well Rosie, I know they have no answers for the spinning of the car, or the fluttering around my head. They can't explain you swimming to me or for helping me out of the ditch. No one claimed you and no one wanted me.

When the intake worker stopped talking, Charlie declared, "I don't even know what you are talking about.

"I think they called the police on both of us. I don't see why they'd have called them on me, but the police did come.

"They came and they hauled us both off, her and me. I told them the dog was mine, but honestly, I really have no idea where she came from.

"Rosie went with the animal control officer and I went to jail.

"I don't know what type of place they took her to, but mine was awful, and I was really sick."

"If it hadn't been for that ditch, I would have never met Rosie. Traveling in a busted up car with a broken windshield, possibly to my death. If that car hadn't landed in that ditch, I would've just kept driving into something else or someone else.

"I sure as hell wouldn't have been in this evaluation, we both know that.

"Again I must confront the question. Am I an addict?"

PART VI: CONFRONTATION

CHAPTER 17: DETOX COMPLETE

Claire's First Visit

was starting to feel like my head was on straight. I had given up the president's mission as something that was simply crazy. My choice now was whether to move on to a treatment facility or just sign myself out. I still had a court hearing on Joe's assault charge, but that could wait. It could wait because today, for the first time since the beginning of this month-long incident, Claire was coming to visit. My God, I was so excited about that. It is going to be wonderful to hug Claire. The staff nurse came by and informed me that Claire was now in the visitation room. I entered the room, and one look at Claire swept my heart away. I sat down beside her and leaned in to give her a hug. Immediately, she pulled away, barely touching me.

"Where's Emma?" I asked.

"She's with my dad," Claire replied.

"Thank you so much for coming to see me."

"We need to talk," Claire said. "I cannot do this anymore. Just listen for once, Charlie, would you without interrupting? Just listen to what I have to say, please."

I tried to speak, but Claire silenced me with the raising of her hand. "It is time for me to speak, Charlie."

"This has affected me deeply. I am worried sick about your next drink and where it might lead. This is tearing me up inside and bringing up such painful memories of my childhood. This is not an environment that I want to raise our child in. This is not healthy for you or me and it is certainly not healthy for Emma."

"No, let me speak Charlie," Claire interjected, as I once again tried to interrupt her.

"I'm frustrated and I'm upset. You had some sobriety and you didn't take it seriously, not seriously enough to stick with it. I know that you've had a lot on your plate with the tornado, your dad's death, and our new baby."

"But sobriety has to come first. I've been going to Al-Anon meetings, Charlie, and I'm learning to make choices for my life. If you're using and drinking, Charlie, then you're not being honest to your program. Most importantly, you are not being honest with yourself."

"Your self-pity is problematic."

"Your anger is driving you back to using. I won't put up with it anymore. That's simply the way it is. That's the way it has to be. Anger is a luxury you can't afford."

"My suffering has been daily and has been going on for years now. At first it was the two of us drinking and using together, but I grew out of that. Now, I need you to work a program. I need you to declare yourself in recovery.

"Each time we've gone through something, a change of job, change of life, I thought, this will be the time that Charlie will commit to sobriety. Every time, I've been disappointed because that has not happened.

"I've given you a lot. I've earned the money. I've covered for you, repeatedly. I've lied for you. Oh, he's sick today. I'm not doing that anymore. I'm so deeply ashamed of your actions, Charlie, that I'm struggling to even hold my own head up.

"How could you attack my father?

"The last time you started drinking, I begged you not to. I begged you. And you snuck around and did it anyway. Then you ran away, and I was terrified that you'd be hurt or that something bad would happen to you. I won't live this way anymore.

"You've made our home a nightmare of twisted turns and manipulations. You had one goal in mind. You wanted to be able to use and drink. This is making me crazy, Charlie. It has got to stop. One of us has to be mature enough to end this madness.

"We have a baby to take care of now Charlie... WE. This isn't just my responsibility."

Charlie interrupts, "Is this about that guy you used to date, David? Is that his name? Are you seeing him again?"

"My God, Charlie, are you completely stupid? Are you even listening to me? I just told you what this is about. This is about your using, period.

"You always try to derail something as if it's not about you. This is all about you Charlie, you and your addiction."

"Stop using distractions. Stop trying to hide your addiction and emotionally confuse me. You just go back to using, and I won't allow it anymore."

"So you don't love me anymore?", Charlie said.

"I won't tolerate your using anymore, Charlie. My love is clouded by exhaustion and emotional pain. I'm not even going to respond to that right now.

"You need to focus on you. You need to get your act together, Charlie."

"Claire, should I go to treatment? Just tell me what to do!" Charlie said

"Well, you're not coming home with me today, I'll tell you that. I refuse to welcome this behavior in my home. I don't want to worry about what my friends might see if they drop by. I'm not going to worry about it, Charlie, because you won't be there drinking and drugging anymore. Not in my home! I will always have hope for you, I just cannot save you. Please, don't quit trying before the miracle happens. This can only work, if you work. You make an effort.

"We have a new baby, Charlie, and I still can't go back to work. Our checking account is drained because of you. I don't even know if I can keep our car insurance, after your accident. If it weren't for Dad helping me, Emma and I would be on the street. We'd be homeless, Charlie, homeless!

"I just can't live this way."

"The Sheriff's department called me two weeks ago and told me they'd found you and had you secure. That's when my fear lifted and my disappointment crept back in. I feel so alone.

"That creepy guy, Jerry, came by; your dealer friend. I can't have people like that at our house or in our life. Emma and I deserve better.

"Do you even remember hitting my dad? Do you remember throwing the vase through the window before you got in your car and ran away?"

Charlie just hung his head. He said nothing.

"Charlie, I feel like you're a reflection of me. My failure if I put up with this. I now have to be the provider for Emma, all by myself."

"You've shown me repeatedly that your addiction is your priority. Your disease is progressing, taken over you. I can't trust what you might do next. You've pulled yourself together more than once, but each time you fall backwards even farther. This time is the absolute worst.

"Charlie, you've been to treatment. I'm not going to keep doing this until you kill yourself. If these are the choices you want to continue to make, you'll be making them on your own.

"I'm smart enough to know that you'll convince me to go back into your arms. You'll be loving and sweet and go through treatment and make a new start, again. But then the hammer will fall, like it always does, and you'll take a drink and you'll have yet another excuse and then we'll be right back here again. You always have some reason to justify your drinking.

"When you're drunk, I feel like I've made the biggest mistake of my life by marrying you. You become a completely different person. I re-live my childhood memories due to my dad's drinking. I have a physical and emotional response that kicks in, even if I don't recognize, see it coming, or even understand myself.

"Maybe it's like your own struggles with your Dad. I really don't know the answer to those things. You'll have to figure them out for yourself.

"If this isn't your bottom and your surrender, then your bottom will be in a cemetery. Charlie, I want to be absolutely clear, I will not go any lower."

And with that, Claire, walked out of the room. I only had myself and to blame. I lost it.

CHAPTER 18: TREATMENT

I woke up in treatment, realizing that drugs and alcohol were no longer there to redeem me, or stop the pain of my guilt and shame. Nor were they there to help control my anger and rage or assist in the reduction of my anxiety. I was engaged in my own personal battle and I was a long ways from the poppy fields of Afghanistan. My unmanageable life was spinning downward and my thought that I could drink again had brought me to the brink of tragedy. The irony and pain that this happened at the same time that I lost my father, and became a father myself, had not escaped me.

I was faced with the unredeemable reality that I had hurt others and I was not forgiven. Still, I must move on. Claire had not forgiven nor forgotten my relapse. The disappointment I saw in her eyes tugged at my heart.

I had relapsed. As a newly recovering alcoholic and drug addict, I had been living with the false assumption that I could now handle using. My assumption was that being cleared of any current drunken offenses, I had self-corrected enough; I had dropped my addictive behavior and self-centered ways. Once again, John Barleycorn had seduced me into just one drink. I nearly paid for that one drink with my life. My therapist told me I may be too smart to live. "It is a simple program, son. Simple. Read Chapter 5 in the Big Book again." (Big Book of Alcoholics Anonymous).

Claire's expectation was that I get into Alcoholic Anonymous. In her voice, I did not hear acceptance. I heard resolution. In her voice, I did not hear forgiveness. I heard her resolve to close any revolving door of perpetual relapse. I heard disbelief and shock that I was aggressive with her father. I did sense a soft hint of love.

If I live the rest of my life unforgiven, expecting to move my life forward, then I have got to get past this self-pity. I can no longer live a life of denial, thinking I am not an addict or that my addiction affects no one but me. I have to get past all the resentment that drives me to drink. My family may not choose to forgive or accept me. They may choose, instead, to remember all my wrongdoings, but I am choosing to stay sober. I want to move forward. I feel confident that I will not be allowed to live further in this fashion; that I will bring myself to an end. Which means that I have to try sobriety. If not, my higher power will take me home. I am sure.

I cannot allow myself the luxury of thinking I can have one beer. I simply cannot allow that to take place or I will lose.

How could I have ever considered that I was not powerless over addiction? How could I have ever considered that I had a choice? From Claire's perspective, I had to commit for the rest of my life not to drink or use drugs. From where I was, staying sober today was a damn good idea because my life had just been devastated again, completely and utterly devastated. Progress, I told myself, not perfection.

Claire was right. I am not like other people. I am not like Robert, who can take or leave alcohol. I am more like my dad, who was totally out of control.

I am not a normal user. I am a fortunate person whose addiction has not yet killed them.

Charlie's mind slipped back to his first week of treatment at the SEK Addiction Treatment Center in Girard. Those days were sunny and almost too warm to be outside, but he enjoyed it there. Charlie sat hidden away from anyone at the facility, at a picnic table, that was neatly tucked around a corner, in the far back. No fellow consumers, no staff. No one could see him at all. He sat with Rosie, and he liked that. They had been there together as he wrote in his journal for hours. He would write and read to Rosie. "I am committed to stay here and engage in treatment through both signature and spoken word. I so promise to my family and, most importantly, to myself.

"The only time I have surrendered was when I was spinning out in my car. I was spinning out of control and that fluttering was going on around my head. At that point, something took over me spiritually, and brought me to safety. That is what I need to focus on now, I need to remind myself of that complete surrender."

Kent R. Leon, Ph.D., LCAC, was Charlie's clinical therapist. He was seventy-plus and to say he was eccentric was putting it mildly. Dr. Leon had been brought back from retirement because Charlie had said he wanted to go to the community-based treatment facility where his mother, Liza worked. The Veteran Affairs Office and local Medical Director had given approval, with the instruction that no one who knew family or who were family could provide any direct care.

Dr. Leon's treatment approach to addiction was based on a book he wrote about twelve step work in AA. His book was based on real life peoples' stories, described through a prism of Gestalt and Existential Philosophy. The cornerstone of his warrior approach followed the teaching of a Rabbi born over 2,000 years ago, Jesus. Leon was also a follower of Ram Dass, the author of the seminal 1971 best-selling book *Be Here Now*. Effective, outrageous, and kind were all words that described Dr. Leon. The man had retired fourteen years prior and had actually treated Joe and Skippy. Charlie laughed to himself, as he had Joe's antique journal to match his antique therapist.

That old expression that time will heal all wounds seemed so distant. It seemed to be a million years away.

Now, here Charlie sat alone with Rosie on a picnic bench trying to complete his writing assignment in the journal.

Old Leon had instructed Charlie to write in his journal the answer to this question: "What is the sound of one hand clapping?"

Charlie wrote his answer as, "The sound of a drunken man who cannot hit his ass with both hands at the same time."

The next journal entry was to answer, "How did your life become unmanageable?"

After that, the instructions were to complete the following four statements:

I resent...

I demand...

I appreciate...

I want...

The second and third questions came pretty easy and were very lengthy entries in Charlie's journal.

The sound of one hand clapping, not so good. Old Leon just laughed and handed Charlie a huge queen conch shell. "You need to try again, my son, you're not listening."

The other questions I did okay on, but now I had to redo all of them with "How I resent," "How I demand" and so on because Old Leon said, "I answered why and not how. That just screws with your head."

"No wonder you got drunk if you treat yourself like that," Dr. Leon admonished me. "The action son. How did you choose? Shit or ice cream, they both look the same. Which would you rather eat? How they taste, the results from each, that's what is different. No one cares why, son. How. That is the key; the behavior action equals the results."

Dr. Leon was a purist in Gestalt Therapy techniques and never asked a patient why, only how. His use of the empty chair was well known.

The next day's session brought the assignment, "What is stopping you from staying sober?" To answer I have to make a list of the worst things that could happen to me if I stay in recovery. I took another crack at the one hand clapping and was told to put the sea shell to Rosie's ear as I was again overthinking my answer. Old Leon is super odd.

The third day I was encouraged to write letters to those I need to make amends to. My instruction was to write a letter to Joe, so that I can read my honesty.

On the fourth day Dr. Leon told me to say ten times, "Pride and memory had a fight and pride always wins." Then read Chapter 5 (Big Book of AA), then rewrite the letter to Joe.

Again Old Leon asked me, "Can you give yourself to this simple program?"

According to Claire, it is time for a big change, and I do agree. There is no redemption for what I have been through and all I have done. There is only hope.

My life was on hold, a pause. I was glad to be able to receive visits from people, now that I had transitioned to primary care, but not everyone was glad to see me. My Uncle Jess was prickly. My whole family were responding to their own frustrations and fears. They had thought I was lost; that I was a dead man this time. I could hear their belief that the next time I would be. My life was going to be what I made of it, and I was fortunate that I had not killed myself spinning out on that overpass.

Just like the night she swam to save me, Rosie never left my side. She was always present, with a capital P. I know this sounds weird, but I read my journal out loud to her. I can sense Rosie's distress when the shit I write is too deep. When I read Joe's journal entry, "The world is only the visible aspect of God. What being a warrior does is cause a challenge by following the trail in search of a higher purpose for a life," she whined and laid her head on my lap.

The night of the accident, Rosie's appearance brought the visible aspect of God to my door. She brought light on my darkest night. I read the reports, actually rewrote them in my journal, but I still do not recall my priestly crossing of the thirty semi-trucks. I remember the fluttering, because it was so physical. I remember Rosie swimming to me in the car as it went under, because it was also so physical. Yes, I thought she was Zoey. The rest is still a blackout that I cannot recall. As these thoughts poured through my mind, Rosie snuggled up even closer to me. She was my little piece of the visible aspect of God.

Dr. Leon looked across the room at the young man, Charlie. The bruising on his face was fading. He was shaven, with a fresh military hair cut; rather nice looking lad.

"It has been five weeks since your wreck, Charlie. You have been with me in treatment fourteen days now, son."

"Right," Charlie said. "If you say so."

"I think it is time to talk about your reoccurring dream. I understand you're waking at night and sitting with the dog."

Breathing in deeply Charlie said, "We don't have to talk about it now."

His heart began to race and his palms began to sweat, Charlie muttered, "Not if you don't want to, I mean it is just a dream."

Silence came over the room. Only the sound of Rosie snoring at his feet could be heard.

"Charlie, you know you're different. You know that the Addiction Treatment Center took you in for recovery, and that I agreed to be your therapist," Dr. Leon said.

Charlie said nothing.

Dr. Leon continued with a voice of kind wisdom, "You had worthy military service, in which you experienced trauma. This continues in your dreams to be unfinished. I say this out of my knowledge and experience treating reoccurring dreams. You were a medic, a healer, and you came upon a soldier who, by no fault of your own could not be healed. He was dead. Beneath him lay a living child. Am I correct?"

Charlie nodded his head.

"Out there I believe is still the family of the soldier, Michael B. Lee, and a little Afghan girl." Dr. Leon paused.

Charlie shrugged. "So, I mean, this is war. I have many veteran and soldier friends. Some are dead, some are alive: life goes on. Whatever."

Dr. Leon said, "In your wreck, son, you could have been killed. That you were not killed was due to chance and the intervention of a dog." Charlie listened. "You are alive, son, and with a life comes infinite potential."

Charlie bursted out, "Why do you keep calling me son? I am not your son."

"I am old; you are young. I call you son. I am a warrior. I interact with purpose. You would do yourself a big favor by asking how and not why."

"How do you call me son?" replied Charlie snidely.

Leon smiled. "Obviously with my voice to your ear. Your assignment is to write two letters: one to the little girl, the other to the family of Michael B. Lee."

Charlie exhaled and as tears welled in his eyes and said

softly, "I have no address." .

Dr. Leon explained, "And you have no letters. Please, first things first."

Charlie shouted, "Damn you," and slammed the door as he walked out.

The next day, Charlie arrived early for his session. He had two letters in hand and an answer for "What is the sound of one hand clapping?"

"The sound of the sea."

Dr. Leon shook his head from side to side. "No. I will look at the letters now."

"Michael B. Lee. Are you certain his family still is out there?" asked Charlie.

Dr. Leon said, "Yes, of course. There is absolutely some living relative."

Then Charlie said, "I want to find them. I figure there is a paper trail for Michael; possibly not for the girl. I am going to try."

Leon instructed: "Next time you have that reoccurring dream, finish the trauma dream with your resolution dream. For examples your search for the family, finding them, the meeting, and then resolution to Michael's relatives. Does this also dominate your daytime thoughts?"

Charlie responded, "Depends. It can, but it is often triggered by an event, even a smell sometimes will trigger it."

Dr. Leon asked, "Lets talk about tranquil positive memories that you have."

Charlie spoke of fishing at the lake as a child.

Dr. Leon explained, "Okay, here is what we will do. Trauma creeps in, we shall knock it out. Close your eyes and visualize a stop sign. Scream STOP. Again. AGAIN. AGAIN!

Remember the physical feel of your face and jaw. Again. Again."

Charlie yelled stop until he was hoarse.

Now, Leon said, "Feel and do the same with no sound. Okay I think you got the first part. Now, pick a specific lake memory. Got it? Charlie, I want you to yell stop. No sound. Start the lake memory. Boom. Again, yell stop in your head. Feel it happen. Boom. Lake memory.

"Do this to stop the intruding thoughts. Every time it starts, every time it returns. Every time knock it out! Knock it out and start the good," Leon said, with encouragement.

"Look for Michael's family. That is fine. Just monitor your body for anxiety and negative thoughts. A warrior knows their spot and higher power. This is about your thinking spot. Physical spots are important as well. People understand getting up and moving around to be comfortable. This is an emotional and mental move in your thinking and habits."

Charlie wrote in his journal, "This time, I have to get this right. There may not be a next time. One day at a time, let go and let God be my constant companion."

EPILOGUE

Reflecting on the car ride home from Rosie's funeral, I began to flip through my journal and look at my notes. Rereading the entries from Skippy, from Joe, plus my own; helps me to follow the Trail of the Warrior and maintain my sobriety. Initially, treatment had been rough. The realization that I was the one that caused not only misery for myself, but for my family as well.

Using drugs and drinking had crept up on me and I had not realized it was going to take me by the throat. I had not realized I was going to keep using to the point of destruction.

If anything was true about the mirror that Claire held up in front of me with her confrontation, it was that I was absolutely powerless and unmanageable. When I finally surrendered, I made a list of what was stopping me from being sober. It was a long list. It included my childhood, the trauma from my time as a medic in the war, as well as from working recovery efforts after the Joplin tornado. It was a lot of things and I listed them all out in my journal. These no longer could be excuses fueling my denial.

That journal saved me, as much as the Big Book. Through the journal, I witnessed Skip's journey as well as Joe's. It gave me hope and the strength to fully surrender and trust, knowing that following the Trail of the Warrior would lead me to sobriety. As much as Rosie had saved my life, the journal restored me back to living.

By the time I left the Addiction Treatment Center, I had realized that a Warrior can heal with a touch or with words.

It was now my duty to share the love of Rosie and the power of the journal. I left Rosie at the treatment center that day, because she did not really belong with me, she belonged with those who needed her help to find their own surrender. The healing words I left behind were found in Rosie's journal. Others could find their surrender and strength following their own trails, and it would do the most good if it was shared, like Rosie's love, during their treatment.

"I love you. Thanks for coming with me today," I said to Claire as she drove us home.

"Are you sure you do not want us to go with you to the Humane Society? We can help you and Liza adopt a new dog," Claire said.

"No, the baby needs to sleep. It is past her nap time."

I grabbed Claire's hand and gave it a squeeze.

I sent up a silent, "Thank you, God," for sending me Rosie

at the time in my life when I needed most her. The moment I thought I had lost everything that I held dear, was the moment I gained every thing I needed.

Rosie had given me the strength to surrender, and now I can celebrate my years of sobriety with my beautiful wife, Claire, and our two daughters.

I have repaired my relationship with Liza and Joe. They both know the struggle I went through, having been there themselves.

Every day I wake up grateful for my recovery, my family, and my sobriety.

I am grateful for everything that led me to the Trail of the Warrior and gave me the ability to stay on that path.

"Claire!" Charlie exclaimed excitedly, "I got it. I finally got it! The sound of one hand clapping is the sound of listening to yourself hear."

DISCUSSION QUESTIONS

1. Who stands out as heroes and heroines? What is it about them that you admire?

2. What is Liza a victim of?

3. What changed first: Liza's thinking or her behavior by being sober? Why is this distinction important and how does it apply to your own situation?

4. Are substance problems a symptom or the cause of domestic violence? What leads you to your conclusion?

5. Who do you identify most with as a character? Why?

6. When it comes to Rosie, how do you see her? How would she be helpful to you in recovery? Is this true of all pets or was she unique?

7. If Charlie were your son or Claire your daughter, how would that feel? How would you have handled the relationship?

8. How is Jess stuck in his emotional state? In what ways do you get stuck in emotional states?

9. Marriage is a challenging reality for any couple. Can a marriage survive addiction? What factors help a marriage survive and what factors get in the way of survival?

10. What could Joe or any characters have done sooner to help save Charlie? At what point would you have intervened and why?

11. What did you see in the mind of the victim as they detox? What has been your experience?

12. Experiencing abuse as a child can be life changing and long lasting. Once the abused child becomes an adult, would you still consider them a victim?

13. Zoe was an integral part of Charlie's life. In what ways did Zoe influence Charlie's life? Have you ever experienced that type of relationship with a pet?

14. What perspective do you consider most valuable in Rosie? Was she more spiritual, more magical, or simply present? And why?

15. What has been your experience with counselors? What have you found most helpful?

16. What was the turning point for Charlie? What has been your turning point?

17. If you were in Charlie's shoes, would you contact Michael's Family? Why or why not? What would you hope to accomplish if you did?

18. Who would most benefit from reading this book? Is the Trail of the Warrior for addicts only or would it appeal to non-addicts as well? How might it be helpful to both?

19. What does the theme of "find your higher power" mean to you?

20. Considering the fourteen trails of the warrior listed, is one trail more worthy of discussion or contemplation? Can you be a warrior without any of the trails?

ACKNOWLEDGEMENTS

A s a story teller, I believe the highest levels of truth are the lessons expressed by our hearts to each other as human spirits. We are the most powerful when we teach a lesson that captures our voice and as that voice heals.

The first acknowledgment is to the four individuals who lent their true life stories to become the voice of the Trail of the Warrior. I am indebted to your for your life teaching gifts and I understand why you must stay anonymous. For all that you have taught me, you have my admiration and respect.

Edits to clarify and strengthen characters were performed by Stacey Hauck, Heather Spaur, Diane Potts, Jerry Davenport, Benjamin Pfeiffer, Ernie Thompson, Peggy Bennet, Robert Richmond, Amy Glines, Michelle York, Jason Wilson, Lynette Downing, Marsha Wallace, Ron Womble, Kent and Debbie Noble, Ray and Mary Atkinson. Graphic Art by Brandon Spaur. Cover Model Tyler Krei.

My appreciation and heartfelt gratitude goes to everyone who supported, encouraged, and helped with the endeavor.

Rosie, who is our beautiful chocolate lab: We all thank you!

ABOUT THE AUTHOR

R.H. Pfeiffer *was born in Fort Scott, Kansas in the 1950s.* Trail of the Warrior *is the third book the author has written, and the author's first published work; earlier works include the manuscripts* Love Against Love *and* Candles Fire and Flame.

The story in Trail of the Warrior *was written over the past three years and is based on a fictional blend of the author's life, friends, and colleagues.*

The core concept of Trail of the Warrior *is a stream of consciousness from R.H.'s life in recovery and service from the last forty-two years. Written with the inspiration of a dog, the seeking of a restless soul for a higher power, and the love and support of colleagues.*

As a storyteller R.H. believes the highest level of truths are the lessons our lives express by the heart to each other as human spirits. We are the most powerful when we have a teaching that captures our voice as it heals.

This book is that voice that illuminates the Trail of a Warrior.

Proceeds from the sale of this book go toward building a new addition treatment center. Thank you for your support.

Limited distribution of this book is available, so order your copy online today at www.trailofthewarrior.com.
$15 per book (plus $5 shipping and handling) to:

Families and Children Together (FACT, Inc.)
911 E Centennial
Pittsburg, KS 66762

Include your name and the address of where to ship.

Connect with R.H. Pfeiffer

Facebook @ Trail of the Warrior by R.H. Pfeiffer
Twitter & Instagram: @rh_pfeiffer
rhpfeiffer@trailofthewarrior.com